Married to a Boss, Pregnant by my Ex 3

Lock Down Publications and Ca$h Presents
Married to a Boss, Pregnant by my Ex 3
A Novel by *Destiny Skai & Chris Green*

Lock Down Publications
P.O. Box 870494
Mesquite, Tx 75187

Visit our website
www.lockdownpublications.com

Lock Down Publications
Like our page on Facebook: Lock Down Publications
@
www.facebook.com/lockdownpublications.ldp
Cover design and layout by: **Dynasty Cover Me**
Book interior design by: **Shawn Walker**
Edited by**: Kiera Northington**

Stay Connected with Us!

Text **LOCKDOWN** to 22828 to stay up-to-date with new releases, sneak peeks, contests and more…

Acknowledgements

This is a career I never understood. I didn't feel books would be the path that I chose, but now I can honestly say this profession has grasped me by the heart. My dedication for this book goes out to my love, Destiny Skai. You are my air and my motivation to push beyond the normal heights. You are a queen of many talents and my life is incomplete without your love and support. Your pen is a beast too, so I would literally go crazy if there wasn't any more Destiny Skai and Chris Green novels.

I would like to thank my brothers, Nathaniel Wilkins aka Nip, and Robert Bell aka Nation Ali. You guys push me to be better with my talent and anger. I do it for all of you boys. My brother Deangelo, my daughter Cerenity, my brother Marquise Rice aka Wildchild and my mother Dolsellia. My family period. The entire Green bloodline. I want to thank everybody who supports the OsaGang movement. May Allah reward you with joy and many blessings. My life is taking a turn and soon I will be walking out of these doors to my freedom. I love all my readers who purchased a Chris Green novel. Also, the fans who supports my love, Destiny. Shout out to LDP for signing two dope-ass authors who refuse to quit. Stay tuned because there's more coming soon. Peace and Asalamulaikum.

Destiny Skai & Chris Green

Chapter 1

One month later 7:30 a.m.

Tossing and turning under the sheets, the sound of Storm's phone ringing broke Dominic from his peaceful sleep.

"Are you gonna answer that?" he mumbled before opening his eyes.

Realizing she wasn't in the bed, he sat up and ran his hand through his deep waves. The water from the bathroom shower was pumping heavy steam into the bedroom and the heat was just a bit overbearing. Just as he reached for the cellphone and pressed the accept button, the incoming caller hung up the phone.

"Hello? Hello?" he spoke through the line, before looking at the main screen. The number read "unknown," so calling back was obviously out of the question.

Shrugging his shoulders, he placed it back on the dresser. After resting his head back on the large cotton pillow, the slight sound of Storm moaning caressed his eardrum. Quickly leaning back up, he figured his mind could have been playing tricks on him. Especially after the drinking game they entertained each other with last night. Unfortunately, the liquor was far gone from his system and the only thing he had to show for it was a brain thumping headache.

Tossing the sheets from his body, he rose to his feet and headed for the bathroom. The small moans escaping from his woman's mouth began to rise as he moved closer. Putting his hand on the door, he pushed it open slowly and stepped inside. Pausing in shock, he nearly collapsed to the floor. The foggy shower glass and steam covering the room couldn't hide Storm being held by the man who pumped forcefully inside her tight kitty.

"Storm! What the fuck are you doing?" Dominic raged, with murder written in his eyes.

Her pupils locked in as Gotti continued to stroke as if he wasn't standing there. "I'm sorry, baby. I can't let him go. I just can't let him go," she spoke through her long gasp of pleasure.

Jumping up from his sleep, Dominic panted heavily. The sound of the warm shower water flowed through their bedroom and the horrible dream that just scared him nearly to death started to feel like déjà vu. Before he could climb out of the bed, Storm's phone began to vibrate loudly. Looking around for a few seconds, he quickly picked up her cell. The mysterious unknown number was back on the screen and he was sure a dream wasn't the reason he was reliving the nightmare that just occurred. Sliding the green button, he placed his ear to the line. "Who is this?"

"Bitch nigga, you know who the fuck this is! Where the fuck is Storm?"

Balling up his face in disgust, Dominic shook his head. "How in the fuck did you get this number? I thought she made it clear to you there wasn't anything to talk about."

"What! You must think yo ass can't get blasted or some. I wanna see my daughter, boy. I'm not playing with you or that bitch about my seed. Now, I been very patient with y'all. The first time I knocked yo ass out in front of ya people. I could've blew ya brains out and sent you to ya maker. The next time, you might not be so lucky," Gotti's voice boomed with hostility.

Looking up at Storm, who strolled out of the bathroom with a towel wrapped around her body, Dominic smirked before placing the call on speaker.

"Listen, O.J. Simpson. Storm isn't trying to talk or have any dealings with you. You're gonna make the *Guinness Book of World Records* for the best stalker of 2019, if you don't quit while you're ahead. There's nothing else left for you to chase, besides a casket. Maybe when you cough up my four hundred grand, we can try to get you some video chat time with Rain, lame-ass nigga."

"How did he get my number?" Storm whispered as her heart began to race while moving close to Dominic's side.

Taking a step back, he brushed off her question with a slight mug. The terrible dream was pumping through his brain and her mouth running wasn't making shit better. Moving towards the bedroom window, he stared out into the bright sun rays before clearing his throat.

"I've been very lenient with you, bro. You've stepped past your boundaries on more than one occasion and I let that shit slide off my back like a G. I'm beyond the business man stage with you. This shit is going too far and you're starting to become a pest," Dominic hissed.

"Let me see the phone, baby. I'll just change the number." Storm offered to kill the entire argument.

Gotti had been lurking around for the past month to get closer to Storm. It was never truly about the child. His selfish and psychotic ways were starting to get even crazier, especially after she slowed down on hanging with the girls. It was always his easy route to slide through and definitely his course with finding out the latest on her whereabouts.

"Why? He's only gonna keep doing this shit. I'm tired. Either this stops or I'm gonna end it myself."

"Put that bitch on the phone, nigga. You acting like a hoe. What, you mad I skeeted in that lil pussy and had a child, huh? You mad cuz she will never deny me no matter how hard you try to keep her away. All I need is ten minutes and she'll be sneaking out of the house to come meet up with me. You probably still have visions of me beating that shit down. Don't make me hunt y'all down and kill you in front of her. Last chance. Put my baby mama on the hook."

Containing his emotions, Dominic clutched the phone tightly.

"There's no need for you to talk to her, because she has nothing to say. That was your last time threatening me and my wife. When I catch yo bitch ass, you better bust ya gun or die. And by the way, that's my daughter now. So you got even more of a reason to commit suicide, before I get word on where you falling asleep at, fuck-boy."

Hanging up, he handed Storm the phone and crossed his arms.

"How did that nigga get your number? And it's not just a coincidence he pressed every damn button on the keypad until it found you."

"I don't know, Dominic. I didn't give it to him, if that's what you're implicating. The only person who has my number is Tia."

"And what about Kendra?"

"I haven't spoken to Kendra ever since you told me not to. Please don't start with me."

"If you ask me, I think both of they asses shady."

"So, what do you want me to do, Dominic? Just cut off all my friends and be confined to this house forever? I guess my life is just meaningless."

Opening the bedroom door, he looked at her with a heated expression. "Start looking somewhere else for us to move."

***

Sitting on the couch with his young squeeze directly next to him, Gotti dialed Kendra's number repeatedly. The threats that Dominic issued was surely about to cause a disturbance he wasn't ready to see. The thought of his daughter being around the clown is what raged him even more. Just on the strength of his disrespectful ass mouth, he would die and Storm could be buried in the darkest tunnel next to him.

"Why you ain't paying me no attention? I been waiting for some dick for the past hour. Why did you even call me over here, Gotti?"

"Bitch, don't you see me handling business? Go and make me a sandwich or some, before I slap yo ass into a new hair appointment."

Watching her stomp off to the back room, he continued to chase down Kendra with no success. The sound of Trel's keys opening his trap spot front door caused him to look up. Standing to his feet, Gotti frowned.

"Nigga, I been blowing yo line up for the past two days, Where the fuck you been?"

Giving him a small shrug, Trel pulled out the money for his recent product and tossed it on the couch. "I just been trying to stay low-key, bro. It's too much fuckery going around and I can't afford to be heading back down to Jackson for another bid. Shit hot, Gotti."

Screwing up his face, he eyed Trel while rubbing the bridge of his nose. "Fuck nigga, what you sign up for? This is the dope game. Not a muffin shop. We sell weight. Everything we do is taking penitentiary chances from the start. You never mind spending that bread you making or driving around in these cars you buying with my money. What's so different now, nigga?"

"It's not the drugs I'm worried about, crazy-ass nigga. It's you. Ever since we been trying to run this business, your nose been stuck inside Storm's ass. We've tried to kidnap this girl, down to killing her husband and it doesn't seem like she's trying to come back. We're gonna end up in prison if you don't focus," Trel stressed, knowing there was more to the story.

"I ain't going back to prison. Not in this life or the next, so you can scratch that shit off your thinking cap. We been moving fine since I came home, so what's the difference now? You making me feel like you're hiding something."

"I ain't hiding shit because it's already known, smart guy. You shot Clyde and didn't handle yo business. That left open room for all the excess drama to fall back on us."

"What the fuck are you talking 'bout?"

"Nigga, Clyde is still alive. He was in a coma and now he's back stable. If that nigga gets his mind right and scream yo name, whoever around you is going down and that can't be me." He replied, handing Gotti the door keys. "I'm sorry, bro. Just hit me when shit has died down."

As Trel walked out of the house, Gotti gritted his teeth before punching a hole through the thin living room wall. The thought of Clyde being alive left doors leading to him. Not to mention, if he ran his mouth to the authorities on the shooting, it was a life sentence waiting to be issued by his racist ass parole officer. Picking up his phone again, he dialed Kendra's number. His heart fluttered after she picked up on the second ring.

"Boy, why the fuck you keep blowing my line up? I'm not interested in no dick right now, Gotti."

"We got a problem. I'm coming over to see you now," he spoke through the line before leaving out of the front door, leaving his chick behind.

Destiny Skai & Chris Green

Chapter 2

Chanel had just arrived at work to start the night shift. As she approached the unoccupied nurse's station, she caught a glimpse of the on-duty cop standing outside of Clyde's room. The detectives on his case provided protection once they received an anonymous tip that someone was trying to harm him. Tossing her purse inside the bottom drawer, Chanel sat her lunch bag underneath the desk and logged into the computer.

The past month had been so stressful that Chanel contemplated about quitting her job every single day, thanks to Trel. True enough, he promised to move her away once she agreed to assist him with the heinous crime, but the situation took a sharp turn and she had to abort the mission. Upon the delivery of the news about the new security on deck, Trel had a fit, placing the blame on her for not moving quick enough.

"Hey, boo."

Chanel turned around to see it was her fellow nurse greeting her with a smile. "Hey, boo. How are the patients tonight?"

"Everyone is resting. I had to dope up Mr. Smith because he kept saying he was in pain and needed a massage."

"A massage?" Chanel giggled. "He think he's at the spa?"

"Chyyy, he think he's at the Asian massage parlor. Talking about he need a happy ending."

"Trisha, stop playing."

"Girl, I'm not. He pulled out that shriveled-up meat and told me to rub it. So I gave his ass an extra dose of Benadryl to knock him out."

"His old ass hung like a horse. That's why he has thirteen damn kids." Chanel burst out in laughter. She was laughing so hard that her eyes started to water. "Well, thanks for doing that, because I'm not in the mood for his nastiness tonight."

Trisha sat down in the cushioned rolling chair beside her. "You know I got you, girl."

"Why you sitting down? Your shift is over," Chanel questioned seeking confirmation.

"I'm doing a double because your help called out again." Trisha smirked and rolled her eyes.

"Damn, that's the third time in a week."

"She a mess, but anyway, Tia was looking for you."

Chanel paused for a moment before replying, "Oh. Did she say what she wanted?"

"No. She just asked if you were on the schedule tonight."

"Oh, okay. I'm about to make my rounds anyway. So, I'll see her in a few."

Trisha stood up and yawned. "Well, I'm going to get me some coffee and use the bathroom. Do you want something?"

Chanel nodded her head. "Bring me a hot French vanilla coffee with two shots of expresso. I had a long night and day."

"I bet you did, fucking around with that young-ass boy." Trisha grabbed her wallet and stood up.

"Hush. Just make sure you use the bathroom before you get my coffee."

"I'll think about it."

Once Trisha was gone, Chanel's phone vibrated. As she looked down at the screen, she smiled after seeing it was Trel.

Zaddy: I love you and I did what we discussed
My Nasty Nurse: I love you too and good
Zaddy: I'm headed home so call me on your break
My Nasty Nurse: K

Chanel smiled because Trel was finally getting away from Gotti. She didn't know him well, but she knew he was nothing but bad news and he brought out the worst in her boyfriend. A tap on the counter caused her to look up and to her surprise, it was the woman that was looking for her.

"Hey, Tia. I was just about to start my rounds."

Tia had a huge smile on her face. "That's okay. I wanted to bring this to you." Raising her arm, she placed a bag on the counter and pushed it towards Chanel.

Chanel was hesitant about taking the gift. "You didn't have to buy me anything."

"Yes, I did." Tia leaned closer to the counter and sat the bag directly in front of her computer. "If it wasn't for you, Clyde would be dead and he certainly wouldn't have a security detail."

"It's my job to make sure my patients are safe and besides, the detective told me to keep my eyes open."

"Well, I appreciate that, so you have to take the gift because I'm giving it to you."

Chanel surrendered with both of her palms up. "Okay. You win. I will keep it."

The White Barn bag had her attention, as she looked inside. There was a variety of hand soaps and a scented candle. "Girl, Peach Bellini is my favorite."

"Lucky guess."

"I love it and thanks again."

"No problem." Tia took a step back from the counter. "I guess we'll see you shortly."

"Yes."

Although she appreciated the gift, Chanel didn't feel like it was deserved. Leaning back in the chair, she thought back to the day she was supposed to end his life.

Chanel stepped inside the small storage closet and closed the door behind her. The anxiety that consumed her body made her palms sweaty and heart race. Rubbing her hands against her snug uniform pants, Chanel fumbled through a few bottles until she stumbled upon the Fentanyl. Grabbing the syringe, she inserted the needle and filled the tube with a lethal dose and put the cap on.

"I can't believe I let him talk me into this shit," she mumbled.

Shoving the empty bottle into her bra, she turned back and grabbed a saline solution bag. Playing it off, she walked out with the bag and went into Clyde's room. The sound of the shower running was music to her ears because that meant Tia was out of the way for a while.

Quickly she rushed towards the bed and sat the bag down. The syringe was in her hand and all she had to do was insert it through his IV. Tia had him tucked completely underneath the blanket, so she pulled it back and grabbed his arm. Her hands trembled terribly as she held the syringe in her hand.

"Come on, Chanel. Get this shit over with," she thought.

After a few deep breaths, she was calm enough to insert the deadly medication. The shakiness of her hands came to a halt and she removed the cap. Slowly inserting the needle, she held her finger on the top. There was no going back once she flooded his system. Her thumb eased down on the top, but she stopped abruptly after seeing a gold jewelry box shimmer in her eye. Once again, her inquisitive nature caused her to look further. Chanel picked up the box and opened it. To her surprise, it was a pregnancy test.

Chanel held onto the bed and gasped for air. It was like her guilty conscience was squeezing her neck, cutting off her air supply. The water from the shower stopped, but Chanel didn't hear a thing. She was still in shock, until she heard the bathroom door close. Jumping from her daze, she slid the top back on and slipped the syringe back into her pocket.

"Hey, Chanel."

"Hey, Tia. How are you?"

"I'm good. Just taking it one day at a time." Tia walked to the bed, so she could see what Chanel was doing. "What's going on?

"I'm about to switch out his IV bag."

"Good. I can't have my baby dehydrating in here."

"No worries. I'm going to take care of him." Picking up the box, she handed it to Tia. "I'm sorry. I'm not trying to be nosey, but it fell when I moved his blanket. You're pregnant?"

"Yes," she said softly.

Tia held the box tightly in her hand as she stared down at it. The sight alone was tugging at her heart, because there was no guarantee that he would make it, which meant he would never know he had a baby on the way.

"I'm so sorry, Tia. I know this is a lot of stress on you, so I'll be praying for your strength."

Tia nodded her head up and down. She was too hurt to reply.

Chanel made sure she put a pep in her step so she could get out of that room quickly as possible. That news was more than she expected and now the guilt was about to kick her ass for sure.

"If you need anything, don't hesitate to reach out."

"Okay."

Chanel rushed out of the room and back to the nurse's station. Fumbling through her purse, she found the detective's card and dialed his number.

"Detective Saunders speaking."

"Hi, Detective. This is Chanel from the hospital. My patient is Clyde Daniels."

"Oh yes. How can I help you?"

"I have a strong feeling that Mr. Daniels is in trouble. There was a young woman here causing a scene and she stated he was going to die regardless. I truly believe his life is in danger."

"Do you have a name?"

"Her name is Toya and she's his ex-girlfriend. I don't have a last name, but it's worth looking into, since she's not happy that he moved on."

"I will check this out and get back with you." Detective Saunders jotted the woman's name in his notepad and tossed it onto the seat.

"Also, is there any way to get an officer to sit with him?"

"Let me make a few calls and I'll see what I can do."

"Thank you so much."

"No problem."

After hanging up the phone, Chanel rushed to the bathroom and flushed the Fentanyl from the syringe. There was no way she could contribute to another child growing up without a father. Firsthand, she had that

terrible experience and she wouldn't wish that on her
worst enemy, let alone an acquaintance.

"Hellooo! Earth to Chanel."

Chanel was out of it for a few minutes, but she wasn't asleep. Going back to that day was like déjà vu all over again. "Sorry. I have a lot on my mind."

Trisha handed her the coffee. "I'm here if you want to talk."

"Thanks, boo. I appreciate that, but I'll be okay."

"Good, 'cause this is about to be a long night."

Chanel sipped her coffee and shook her head. "Tell me about it."

Destiny Skai & Chris Green

Chapter 3

Jumping out of his vehicle, Gotti slammed the door and proceeded up the driveway to Kendra's front door. Using his fist to knock, Kendra quickly snatched open the door before he could continue to beat the paint off. Her robe was slightly open, exposing her smooth, butter pecan skin. The drops of water falling from her crinkled hair were enough to show that she just hopped out of the shower.

"What the fuck is wrong with you? Just because you don't got no damn respect for anyone else, doesn't mean you gonna try me, motherfucker."

"Lower ya tone before I choke yo ass the fuck out." He moved past her into the apartment.

Watching him take a seat on her couch, she huffed before slamming the door. Crossing her arms, she took a seat on the opposite side of him.

"It's early in the morning and you beating a bitch door down, like we about to be raided by the feds or some shit. What's so important?"

"Because we have a problem. Clyde isn't dead."

Cutting her eyes at him, she smirked. "And whose fault would that be?"

"Cut the smart mouth shit, bitch. I know it's my fault. I tried to have enough respect for the family not to shoot the lame-ass nigga in the head. But if you wanna point some fingers, we can point them at you also. I told you to tell those nothing ass thots you work with, to keep a close eye on this man to ensure he doesn't have any chance of that. You agreed. Remember?"

He sat up with a raised eyebrow.

"Nigga. Is you slow or what? The only person I'm close to like that is Tia. That's her man, sir. It wouldn't have worked unless I got another female from a different department to handle it. That's not easy to do. We're talking about murdering someone. That's not the average shit a person is ready to do on a regular day after clocking in. I know you didn't expect me to put my own face on the scene, because that damn sure was not about to happen. You have to relax and let things flow or we'll both end up in prison, Gotti."

Scratching his head, he closed the gap between them. "Please watch the way you talk to me. I've had patience with you, but you're pushing that button. All I'm trying to do is get my family back. This nigga trying to raise my child and Storm is making him feel that it's okay, because she's scared. That's where you come in. You're the only one who can talk some sense into her before it's too late."

"And what gives you that bright idea? Storm is blinded by dick and love. You were supposed to have this girl in your bed, tucked in by now. Instead, you chose to beef with her husband. You need to take your attention off him and focus on sweet talking her back into letting the baby see you."

"Don't you think I've tried that a hundred times? He's blocking harder than a maxi pad on a fresh cycle. If I knew where they slept, I could just kill this boy and end it all."

Hearing the word kill caused Kendra to sit up. "You're not killing him. That's not in the plan. If he dies, the deal is off. You're not the only person on a mission. I still have unfinished business also," she said with a serious expression.

"You talking like there's a better plan in your head. I'm waiting to hear it." Gotti mugged.

"Yes, I do. See, unlike yourself, I prepared for something to go wrong with this. I'm gonna get Storm to come and meet up with me. She's been very distant lately, so I know he's gotten into her head. While you were pressing Jade to do your dirty work, I was too busy following you and Storm snapping a few dirty shots for a little extra comfort. He's an inch away from leaving her."

"And what makes you think that's true?"

"Because he still feels your dick is going inside his woman."

"You mean my woman."

"Whatever." Kendra sighed. "The point is, he doesn't trust her. So, all you have to do is let me worry about her. You need to focus on handling this unfinished business with Clyde. If he talks, you're not gonna be the one happy in the end. A bullet to the head is better than a life sentence in prison, while Dominic is raising Rain."

Thinking on her last statement, Gotti sat puzzled for a slight second. Clyde would definitely cause all hell to break loose if he spoke. A part of him said he would keep it gutta and leave it in the streets. But his hood intuition screamed that Clyde was the biggest pussy in the city when it came down to pistol play. It was truly no way around killing him. Trel was the next in line to be checked. His disappearing act showed fear and too much info had been dispersed between the two of them. There was no room to leave anybody around to talk about the smallest details of his plan. It was only to ensure that he didn't fall.

"I need you to find out what room this nigga is in. I can send my youngin' to pay him a visit before he turns into a canary."

"That shouldn't be hard, but getting in that hospital room is. If he's alive like you say, the authorities will be keeping a close eye out on him, Gotti. Unless your little killer is half Spiderman, you better start forming another plan before it spills overboard," Kendra warned before standing up.

Roaming his eyes down to her cream-colored thighs, he smiled and licked his lips. "Sounds like you got everything planned out just right."

"Just enough to make sure my ass is covered. I'm not into losing anything I'm after. Period."

"That ass ain't covered up at all, if you ask me."

Noticing him taking a peek at her backside, a sneaky smile crept across her face. "Try and keep your mind focused on business, freaky-ass nigga. If you don't mind, I gotta get ready to handle some personal things with a friend. It's time for yo ass to ride out." She smiled before opening the door.

"What personal thing would that be?" Gotti was now standing and moving slowly towards her.

Smacking her lips, she placed a hand on her hips. "Damn. If it's okay with you, I'm about to get some dick, sir. Do I have to get a permission slip signed or something?"

"Nah, but you can tell that nigga to turn his ass around. You already busy."

"Excuse me?" Kendra spat, screwing up her face.

"You heard what the fuck I said." Gotti dropped his pants to the floor, exposing his large boxer brief print.

Looking down at his masterpiece, her mouth hung slightly open before rising to match his lustful gaze. "Gotti, I'm not trying to go there with you. Your hands are already full with Storm. Remember?"

"I'm not asking," he replied, snatching his boxers down.

Feeling her heart rate increase, she closed the door and walked away with him in tow. "You got thirty minutes, nigga." she mumbled while walking into her room.

Smiling, Gotti moved behind her, closing the bedroom door.

***

Stepping out of the hospital's elevator, Detective Saunders moved swiftly towards the private infirmary section and stood in front of the counter. The nurse on duty looked up with a smile.

"May I help you, sir?"

"I'm Detective Saunders and I'm here to see a patient, Mr. Clyde Daniels."

"Yes, sir. Please continue," she spoke with a sweet tone.

"Thank you."

Walking slightly down the hall, he stopped in front of the rookie officer who guarded Clyde's room and flashed his badge. Acknowledging Saunders, he moved to the side, allowing him to enter. The small bed Clyde occupied was sitting right under the large window inside the room. Tia was sitting beside him, caressing his hand while the nurses attended to him. The detective wasted no time getting to the point of his visit.

"Mr. Daniels. It's great to see that you're back with us. We've been waiting for you to awaken. My name is Detective Saunders and I'm the one doing the investigation on your case. We found you pretty banged up, lying next to your grandmother's grave. Do you know who would want to do something like that to you?"

"He's still in a lot of pain, Detective. He's probably going to need a few more days to rest." Tia interfered.

"It's okay, ma. I'm good." Clyde stopped her before she could continue.

His voice was raspy from the long coma he endured and his body was nearly motionless as he breathed calmly. The only thing running through his mind after he awakened was the flashes of Gotti's gun firing towards him. It was one thing to be tormented by his absurd actions, but to nearly have his life ended by his own flesh and blood placed things on a different level.

"Why are you even here, Detective? I mean no disrespect, but if you all would be doing your job the way you suppose to, I wouldn't have to remember anything about that day. I've been laying in a bed for almost two months and nothing has happened to ensure this doesn't happen to me again."

Placing both hands inside his pants pockets, Saunders gave him a curious eye. "I don't know if you're aware of this, Mr. Daniels, but investigating a case takes time and accurate evidence. We can't just go out and arrest a person for a crime if we aren't sure on who's a suspect. I mean, for you to say something like that is out of the ordinary. I could've went off your past criminal history of drug dealing. I know that someone was probably in the mix of robbing you for a few keys of cocaine. Or was it a personal issue? Like a debt?"

Watching Clyde inhale deeply, Saunders knew he hit a soft spot.

"You need to watch your mouth and be careful on how you cooperate with us, Mr. Daniels. I'm here to help you. Not to be against you. But, in order for me to help, you have to let me know what the hell you've mixed yourself into, sir."

"Baby, just tell him whatever he needs to know. Please," Tia begged with a sad facial expression.

Hearing the sadness run through her tone, Clyde made a quick choice. Lowering his gaze, he spoke just above a whisper, "It was Gotti."

Tia's face dropped in shock, hearing his name. "What!"

Stepping closer, Saunders pulled a cellphone from his pocket and held it up. "Can you please repeat that? I need you to be more specific, Mr. Daniels."

"The man who shot me is my cousin. His name is Gotti. That's all I have to say."

"Thank you, Clyde. I promise, we're going to make sure this never happens again. To you or anyone else," Detective Saunders replied before placing a call.

Chapter 4

The words from Jade's letter haunted Storm's every waking moment and it was time to get to the bottom of the letter she left behind. Hooking a left at the stop sign, Storm maneuvered down the street with every intention on beating some ass if shit went south. As soon as she got close up on the residence, she spotted a familiar car parked behind Kendra's car.

"What the fuck is Gotti doing here?" she mumbled.

Contemplating on stopping, she decided against it and kept it pushing. The last thing she needed was a confrontation with the father of her child. Just as she was driving past, the door opened so she hit the gas to make sure no one saw her.

"Calm down. You'll deal with that bitch later."

Storm continued to drive across town for an additional twenty minutes, until she ended up at her next destination. Pulling up in the driveway, her heart started to flutter and regret surfaced instantly. Stepping from the vehicle, she walked across the grass, avoiding the crime scene tape. Using her key to gain entrance, she pushed the door open and slowly stepped inside. The emptiness and coldness sent a chilling feeling down her spine, knowing Jade took her very last breath in the home.

It was clear that there was an investigation because of the way things were tossed around. Storm headed down the hallway and stopped at the bathroom door. Tears started to form in her eyes as she eyeballed the bathtub. A vivid image caused her to envision the way Jade was laid out in the tub and jump back. All she could see was a pool of blood.

Quickly walking away, she went inside Jade's bedroom and stood in front of her dresser. The picture stuck to her mirror grabbed her attention, so she pulled it off. After all that time, she never removed the picture they took at the comedy show prior to their fall out. Her hands trembled because there was no way she could go back in time and correct her wrongs.

Rubbing the picture, she wallowed in sorrow. "I'm so sorry, Jade. I should've given you a chance to apologize. I should've never told you to kill yourself, but now it's too late. This was all my fault. All I want is for you to please forgive me."

Storm stood in place and sobbed loudly. "Jade, if you can hear me, please give me a sign about Kendra, because I don't understand. I'm so lost right now."

Storm wiped the tears from her eyes and stuck the picture in her back pocket. Getting back to the point of her visit, she searched hopelessly through each dresser drawer in hopes that she would find an answer to her question. The dead didn't speak, so she prayed that Jade left something behind that would shed light on what was happening during her absence.

After searching high and low, she came up empty-handed and decided to end the search. As she walked towards the bedroom door, a cold gust of wind caused her to stop and look around nervously.

"Storm, you trippin' and it's time to leave."

Just as she was about to exit, a lightbulb came on in her head, causing her to spin in a half-circle. Heading towards the bed, she raised the blanket and lifted the mattress. As she suspected, there was a large manila envelope. Storm grabbed it and let go of the mattress. Taking a seat on the bed, she opened it and pulled out a nice stack of paperwork. Flipping through the pages, she came across the documents for the house. On the contract was her name listed as a co-signer. Jade's credit wasn't strong enough and being that she saw her as a sister, she decided to help her get the place. The love Storm had for Jade was more than what she possessed for Kendra and Tia. And that was probably the reason she said to look out for her.

As she continued to fumble through papers, a set of bold letters made her heart drop to the pit of her stomach. Storm's hand started to tremble hard like she had a touch of Parkinson's disease. Her breathing increased rapidly. In her hands was a copy of a recently dated police report. Storm read the description line by line and became disgusted when she realized Jade had been sexually assaulted by Gotti. Not only did it happen more than once, but it occurred after his release from prison.

"That no-good son of a bitch."

Storm was baffled and couldn't believe Gotti would cross that line once again and with force at that. It was no secret that he could be a danger to himself and other people, but this incident was far too extreme. Rage and pain tackled her body all at once, as she imagined the torture Jade endured at the hands of her daughter's father. It hurt to know he could do that when he claimed to love her at the same time. Although she was happy with Dominic and wanted no parts of Gotti, that didn't make it hurt any less. Storm pulled her phone from her pocket and shot him a text message that said, *I know what you did and for that, you will never see my daughter. I hate you and I hope you die, you dirty bitch.*

Not one single minute passed before Gotti started to blow up her phone, but she forwarded him to the voicemail. Before she could put her phone away, he sent her a message. *'I don't know what the fuck you talkin' 'bout, but about my daughter I will email Jesus. So stop playin' with me. Pull that shit if you want to and watch I bury yo' ass alive.'*

Unfazed by his threat, Storm closed the message and dialed Tia's number. "Hello," she answered.

"I need to talk to you."

***

"If I do this, you have to agree to stay the fuck away from me and my girl for good. I don't want anything else to do with you after this."

"Come on, Trel. It's me you're talking to. That's my word," Gotti replied before lowering the gun to his side. "I'll meet you outside in two minutes," he added before leaving the scared couple alone.

"We need to get the fuck out of here. That nigga is crazy and this isn't going to end well, Trel," Chantel whispered with her chest heaving quickly.

"Bae, just play along. I got a plan, but I need you to trust me. If I buck on him right now, he's gonna try and hurt you. I wouldn't be able to live with myself if I let something happen to you because of my mistakes."

"Trel, don't go with this man. We can just call the police!"

Placing a hand over her mouth, he pointed a finger towards the front door. "He's probably listening. I need you to watch out for my phone call and stay calm until you hear from me. Do you understand?"

Nodding, Chantel kissed him and locked lips before hugging his neck. Exiting the apartment, Gotti was waiting patiently in the driver seat of his car when he spotted Trel heading for him. Pulling out his cell, he pressed Storm's name and began to type his message. *'I don't know what you have going through your head, but I'll give you one chance to let me have my child. After that, I'll let you breathe. If you buck, I'ma gonna bury you with him. Why do I have to get violent for you to understand? I'll see you soon.'*

Gotti sent the text just as Trel climbed in the car. "After this business is done, you ain't gotta worry 'bout me anymore. I hate to sound selfish, but you really ain't have too much of a choice."

"Whatever you say, Gotti."

Trel's mind was already set on what needed to be done. All he had to do was wait for the perfect time to show Gotti he wasn't the only one with a plan up his sleeve. People of his kind only ended up in two places, a penitentiary or a ditch, where only the crooked cops and bad guys knew about.

* * *

Tossing on his thin white t-shirt, Dominic grabbed his car keys and decided to go ahead and slide down on the last few people of his business and give them a two-week warning. That life was over with. The hustling and boss man status was officially over. After he began dealing with so much of Storm's past, there was no room left to handle anything else. Money was never an issue when it came down to his pockets, but dealing with a clown like Gotti, who wouldn't let his family breathe is where the major problem began to kick in. The heat was a little too hot and focusing on anything but that, could end up with someone getting hurt and there was no room for that.

Tucking a gun on his side, Dominic headed for the door. Just as he stepped out, Detective Juan was preparing to knock.

"Mr. King. It's a pleasure to meet you again. It's been a while." He smirked.

Dominic stood speechless before folding his arms. "Detective Juan. What are you doing here? I haven't seen you since my last court case ten years ago. How did you find my home?"

"Relax, King. My problem isn't with you. I was actually here to see if I could speak to your wife. Is she in?"

Hearing a request to speak with Storm sent curious thoughts through his mind immediately. "Uh. For what? My wife is out running errands right now. If there's some type of problem, I'm sure you can tell me," Dominic replied, while trying to conceal the handle of his weapon.

Spotting his actions, Juan took a step back. "Listen, I have no reason to bother you for anything. But I'm investigating the murder of your wife's friend, Jade. I don't know if you're familiar with her or not."

"I am."

"That's good. So you know and understand my purpose for being here. I don't think her death was just a suicide. I actually think there is a little more to this story. I figured your wife could possibly fill me in on her history with the victim."

"My wife is going through a critical moment right now. We just had our child and she's experiencing a lot of stress right now. Maybe you can leave a card and I'll make her aware of this when she comes home."

Pulling a small card from his pea coat, Juan frowned with a raised brow. "Be sure you do, Mr. King. I would hate to think your drug empire has anything to do with this. Have a good day." Detective Juan said, while walking back towards his truck.

Memories of Dominic's hustling days flashed through his head as Detective Juan climbed in his vehicle to leave. It was the same man that nearly cost him to lose his life at a drug trial and now he'd resurfaced on a different mission. Tension was about to rise and it would be deeper than a street beef between him and Gotti.

Chapter 5

Storm was standing in the kitchen, prepping a bottle for Rain, when Dominic walked in dressed in pajamas. "Good morning, baby."

"Good morning, my king." Storm's eyes zoomed in on his print before tiptoeing and kissing him in the mouth. "No work today?"

Dominic stood at the counter, in front of Rain's seat and played with her tiny hands.

"Me and the princess are going to chill today while you go and talk to Detective Juan. Isn't that right, baby?" Rain cooed and kicked her legs, as if she was responding to his question.

The relationship between the two made her heart smile. A few months ago, she never saw this day in her future. The fact that her husband was able to love his stepchild as his own spoke volumes about his character. And for that, she would love him forever. No one or nothing could come between them again. Not even Gotti. A man like Dominic was like a dream come true.

"Well, I'm jealous," she joked, while tickling the bottom of Rain's foot. "Look at you, pretty girl. Stealing all the attention from daddy."

Storm shook the bottle and handed it to Dominic. "Feeding duty is on you, baby. I'm about to go upstairs and get dressed."

Dominic picked up the baby seat and went into the living room. Rain became cranky and started to have a fit. He quickly began to unstrap her. "Aww. Daddy's baby is upset. Are you hungry, my love?"

Scooping her into his arms, he cradled her close to his chest and put the bottle in her mouth. Immediately, the crying ceased. The sight of her chunky jaws moving rapidly as she sucked on her bottle made him chuckle.

"Somebody was starving." Rain gripped his shirt with her hand and closed her eyes. "God knew exactly what he was doing when he brought you into our lives. I love you like my own and I will protect you at any cost. I promise." Dominic kissed her forehead gently.

***

Two hours later, Storm was clear to leave the police station. When she walked out, it was with a heavy heart and a wet face. Detective Juan opened up a lot of old wounds, while creating new ones to bruise her aching heart. Rumors were one thing, but to see and hear facts elevated that hurt to a higher level.

Inside the truck, Storm took a few deep breaths as the tears continued to stream down her cheeks. Shrill screams of her cellular device cut the silence quickly. Storm fumbled through her purse until she felt it graze her fingertips. Without looking at the screen she answered.

"Hey, baby girl."

"Hey, Dad."

"How are you?" Storm's father, Willie asked.

"Um. I'm okay."

"It doesn't sound like it. Is Dominic treating you right? Has he done something to you?"

"No." Storm shook her head. "Dominic is everything I've ever dreamed of. He would never hurt me." Storm contemplated on telling him the truth, but she knew he wasn't easily persuaded.

Sighing heavily, she leaned against the steering wheel. "It's Jade."

"What did she do this time?" Her father knew Jade had a history of making the worst decisions in life. Then Storm would always be the one to come and clean up her mess.

"Dad," Storm's voice box trembled. "She committed suicide."

Stunned to say the least, he rubbed his temple. "Aww, sweetheart. I'm so sorry to hear that. Why would she do such a thing?"

Speaking softly into the phone, she sniffled. "I don't know."

"Baby, that's why I keep you in my prayers. The world is wicked, more than it has ever been. This generation needs to go to church and pray every day."

Storm knew a sermon was coming, so she decided to put an end to it before it started. "Thanks, Dad. I would love to stay on the phone and chat with you, but I have to go and look at this house."

"You're moving?"

"We're selling the house, so I have to look for another one."

"You should consider moving to Texas. I would love to have my grandbaby close to me."

"We'll think about it."

"Well, I won't hold you up. Tell Dominic I said hello."

"I will. I love you, Daddy."

"I love you too, sweetheart."

After I released the call, I noticed I had a text message, so I opened it. Lo and behold, it was the devil herself.

Kendra: Hey. It's been a while since we've spoken and I think it's time for us to have a sit down and clear the air. If you are up to it, come to our favorite lounge. Lunch is on me.

Storm read that message three times and thought about what Dominic said about staying away from her. Deep down inside, she wanted to take his advice, but the other part of her wanted to reconnect with her friend. They already lost Jade. She didn't want to lose another sister. Closing the message, she dialed Dominic's number.

"Hey, baby. You're finished with the questioning?"

"Yes."

"So you're on your way home?"

"No, not yet. I'm about to meet the realtor and check out a few properties. I'll be home afterwards."

"Okay."

"I love you."

"I love you too," Dominic replied sweetly before hanging up the phone.

Twenty-five minutes later Storm was walking into the lounge. As she looked from left to right, she spotted Kendra sitting in the booth. Sauntering towards the table, Storm slid into the booth and placed both hands in her lap.

"I'm glad you decided to show up."

Seeing Kendra brought out a lot of emotion and she wanted to believe there was no ill intent behind that kiss with Dominic. That the only reason it happened was because of the alcohol. She was praying this situation wasn't similar to Gotti and Jade. Doing her best to remain calm, she swallowed her spit and exhaled.

"A lot has been going on, so I decided laying low was in my best interest."

Kendra huffed, "Is Gotti still causing problems?"

"Just as sure as he's alive," she mumbled.

42

"So what are you going to do about it?"

"Honestly, I don't know. I wanted to give him visitation, but he doesn't want to agree to my terms. He's too focused on the fact that Dominic is with her on a daily basis. That's my husband, so I don't know what he thought was going to happen."

"Well," Kendra stretched that word for dear life. "He was under the impression y'all would be together. I mean, y'all were messing around heavily, so maybe he thought the two of you were going to be a family."

"No. That's not happening. Not in this lifetime or the next."

"You sure about that?"

Storm rolled her neck. "Yes, I'm sure. Gotti has done enough damage to me and I'm done with that part of my life. I'm thinking about getting a restraining order against him."

"Now you know damn well that fool ain't going for that."

"He doesn't have a choice."

Kendra held her hands up to surrender. "Sorry. I'm just saying, but we can talk about something else, since that's a touchy subject."

"Yeah, let's do that."

The waitress walked up to take Storm's order. After ordering a soda, she left the two at the table. "So, what's been going on with you? Have you spoken to Tia?" Kendra asked.

"No. Is she okay?" Storm panicked.

"So that means you don't have the hot tea then."

"What?" Her brow creased downward.

"So you know Gotti's cousin, Clyde, right?"

"Yeah."

"Well apparently, Tia and Clyde are an item. When I was over there, she kept trying to get me to leave because she didn't want me to see who was coming."

"Are you sure? The two of them haven't messed around in years."

Kendra popped her lips together. "Hell yeah. You know my ass nosey as fuck. The detective called to tell her that he was shot. She told him that was her boyfriend. She was crying and all. I'm the one that took her to the hospital."

"Damn!" Storm was shocked. "Is he okay?"

"I guess so. We haven't spoken that much because she's been at that hospital day and night with him."

"Oh, wow. I need to check on her."

"Good luck with that." Kendra sipped on her cocktail. "You sure you don't want a drink?"

"No. I'm good. I need to be sober when I get home." Looking at her phone, she checked the time. "As a matter of fact, I can't stay too long. Dominic has been on daddy duty all day."

"So he's accepted the baby as his?"

"Yes." Storm was ecstatic with her reply. "Dominic has really stepped up and had a change of heart."

"That's good."

"I'll be right back. I'm going to the bathroom."

"Okay."

Kendra watched as Storm walked away and disappeared behind the wall. Reaching into her purse, she pulled out a bottle of Special K, a date-rape drug. Observing her surroundings, she made sure no one was looking before she put a few drops into Storm's glass.

"This bitch must be crazy if she think she's about to live happily ever after while walking in my shoes. I don't think so." Kendra pulled out her phone and sent a text.

Psycho Dick: Get ready

Leak: Yup

Kendra was putting her phone away when Storm came back and sat down. Sipping on her drink, she looked over at someone she once considered a sister and hoped that would make her follow suit. The quicker she drank her soda, the better. The envy and hate she felt towards Storm was far greater than the love she possessed. In her eyes, she was an ungrateful bitch and didn't deserve a man like Dominic. The only person made for her was Gotti and she determined to get them back together.

"Why are you so quiet and distant?" Kendra attempted to make small talk.

"There's so much on my mind and I'm just trying to make sense of it all."

"Let's chat like old times. I'll order you a drink."

"No, it's okay." Storm pulled her glass close to her and stirred the soda, but she didn't take a sip. That pissed Kendra off. The last thing she wanted was the ice to melt.

"Why not? You can't drink anymore since you became a mother? Or did Dominic tell you not to."

"No. I just prefer not to since I'm on mommy duty when I get home." Finally Storm started to sip from her straw and the devil started smiling.

"So tell me why you've been so distant from me." Kendra was pretty certain Dominic told her about the kiss, so she was prepared for that conversation.

"Honestly," she sighed. "At first, it was because I wasn't sure about who was telling Gotti things about me.

He knew shit that only we knew about. Dominic definitely wasn't having a conversation with him about me."

"Well, we established that was all Jade's doing."

"Yeah I get that, but then." Storm paused as she thought of way to drop the bomb that Dominic revealed to her. "Dominic told me about Christmas night."

Kendra put her acting skills on and became quite emotional. "I know what it sounds like, but you have to believe that wasn't intentional. We had been drinking a lot. Then we started talking and I kissed him. Storm, I swear that was an accident. I even apologized to him for crossing that line."

"Okay, well if that's true, why did you sneak into our house when we weren't there? We have cameras, Kendra."

"I know that. Do you really think I would do something shady like that? The only reason I was there was to bring the baby her gifts. No one was there, so I went inside and put the stuff in the closet. If you don't believe me, check the closet in the nursery when you get home."

Storm didn't know what to believe, so she just sat there in silence for a moment, staring at the floor. Finally, she looked over at Kendra. "I truly want to believe you had no ill intentions, but Dominic doesn't feel that way."

"So you don't believe me?"

"That's not what I'm saying, but I do have to take my husband's feelings into consideration."

"I get it. Fuck the fact that you've known me longer and I've never done anything like this before."

Storm grabbed her purse and started to ease out the booth. "You know what, Ken, I have a headache and I can't do this right now. Thanks for lunch, but I'm leaving."

Standing on her feet, she lost her balance and fell back into her seat. Kendra jumped up. "Storm! Are you okay?"

"I don't feel too good."

"Come on. Let me help you."

Kendra dropped some money on the table and pulled Storm up by her arms. Placing her arm around her waist, she escorted her to the door. Other patrons were staring, but no one said a word. Just as they were exiting, the waitress appeared. "Is she okay?"

"She doesn't feel well, but I left more than enough money on the table for the bill and your tip."

"Thank you," she replied and walked away quickly.

Walking through the half-empty parking lot, Kendra spotted Storm's truck parked next to her car. So she proceeded in that direction. Just as she walked up, Gotti emerged from his car and grabbed Storm.

"Baby mama, you okay?" he smiled. "Get her keys and open the door."

Storm's head was spinning heavily, as she realized who was holding her up. "Gotti, let me go."

"I got you, baby, don't worry."

Kendra hit the remote, pulled the back door open and climbed inside. "Put her in and I'll pull her."

Gotti lifted her limp body into the backseat and Kendra pulled her inside. Storm was completely out of it, as they stretched her out across the seat.

"Get in the front," Gotti demanded.

Kendra climbed over the seat and sat on the passenger side. When she turned around, Gotti was leaning over Storm, kissing her lips. "I told you I'll never let you go, but you didn't believe me."

"Fool, you do know she can't hear you?" Kendra rolled her eyes and shook her head.

Gotti cut his eyes at her. "Do you ever shut the fuck up? I see why you don't have a man, goddamn."

"The reason I don't have one is because y'all ain't shit. This dummy waited on you to get out of prison and you still fucked her over." Kendra smirked. "And you was still fucking her best friend wit'cha nasty ass."

"I'm fucking you too. So what's the problem?"

"Not for much longer, you cocky bastard."

Kendra reached into her bra and pulled out a tube. Removing the top, she used the metal stick to scoop up a small amount of cocaine. Placing it close to her nose, she took a hard sniff. Using the back of her hand, she wiped her nose and cleared her throat. Gotti was fondling Storm when she looked over at him.

"Soon enough, I will be fucking your competition. So you better get your bitch on board, before this shit gets ugly."

Gotti had heard enough of Kendra's slick-ass mouth. Reaching across the seat, he hit her in the mouth. "What the fuck's wrong with you?"

"You talk too much shit. Learn to keep those dick suckers closed sometimes damn."

"Make that your last time hitting me."

"Get out. I'll let you know when I'm finished."

"Yeah, whatever." Kendra got out and slammed the door.

Satisfied that she was gone, Gotti adjusted the seats so he could handle his business.

Kendra sat in the car scrolling through Facebook. When her attention shifted towards the truck, she could see it rocking. She already knew what was going down. Granted, she didn't want Gotti, it still pissed her off that he would fuck Storm in her presence. That was not a part of the plan.

"I'll be glad when this is over. I can't stand his nasty ass."

Completely annoyed, she reached back into her bra and pulled out her vial. This time she took two bumps and put it back. Holding the bridge of her nose, she closed her eyes, leaned her head back on the headrest and cleared her throat. Kendra was high and out of her mind. By the second, she was growing annoyed and agitated.

"Time to bring this to an end."

Kendra got out the car and closed the door. The truck was still moving, so she snatched open the passenger door. "Damn, you not done yet?"

Gotti stopped mid-stroke and looked up. "Shut up and take the pictures."

Kendra climbed inside and opened the camera on her phone. Using the flash, she snapped multiple pictures of a passed-out Storm. "If these pictures don't make him leave her, I don't know what will." Laughter erupted from Kendra, as she put her phone away. "Hurry up and let's go before somebody sees us."

Chapter 6

After putting Rain to sleep for her afternoon nap, Dominic glanced at his watch that read four thirty in the afternoon. Checking out a few properties online, he pondered on the houses that Storm headed out to view. Looking around his luxurious home, his head dropped in disappointment. The plan was to move his wife in and to dedicate the world to her. Unfortunately, havoc wrecked their dreams straight into the ground. The vibration of his cell phone interrupted the small thoughts that were dancing around his brain. Viewing Storm's name on the screen, he quickly picked it up.

"Wassup love?"

"Is that how you answer the phone for her? You gotta be the biggest lame in America," Gotti chuckled through the line.

Dominic's adrenaline started to flow after hearing his voice. To be sure that he wasn't dreaming, his eyes rotated back to Storm's name on the cellphone.

"If you put your hands on my wife, I'm gonna find you a new apartment under the concrete." Dominic was now heading to his master bedroom.

Laughing loudly through the receiver, Gotti sparked a cigarette.

"First of all, I'm a playa. I'm not really into the beating women shit. If my hands are placed on Storm, it's because she wanted them there. You know my baby mama can't resist me."

Listening to the ignorance spill from Gotti's mouth, Dominic headed into the closet and grabbed his Beretta handgun. "Nah, nigga. The only thing I know is you've been harassing my wife. You're a pest, a man who's in denial and can't accept rejection. Now I've never been a fan of calling the authorities, so if you plan on doing anything harmful to my woman, I suggest you pull up and handle the situation like a true gangsta."

"Slow ya roll, Captain America. You mean our wife. You ain't gotta worry about nothing, but staying outta sight from me, pops. We just met up to have a little warm sex. So, I thought I would give you a call while she's washing up to see how you been."

Huffing with a small smirk, Dominic posted up in the hallway of his home. "Or maybe you're being a stalker and stole her cellphone. She has no reason to have sex with a little boy when she has a whole man at home. I mean, let's be real. There's no way you think I can't take care of all that pussy on my own."

"Hold on for one sec," Gotti said while pressing a few buttons in his ear. Hearing the notification alert pop on his cellphone, Dominic placed the phone on speaker and clicked on the message from Storm.

"Open that message with caution, old man. I don't need you to have a heart attack."

Ignoring him, Dominic clicked the attachment and instantly lowered his head. Viewing the pictures of Gotti on top of Storm having sexual intercourse was enough to knock the wind from his chest. Pressing the end button on the phone, he slid down the wall and took a seat on the hardwood floor. The pain he was feeling at the time was unbearable. Being a fool for Storm was drowning him in a disastrous pool of love. It was a nightmare that he refused to keep reliving. Now that he was sure about the woman he shared a bed with, he had to make some changes in order to strengthen his heart.

* * *

As Storm slowly opened her eyes, she realized she was sitting in the driver's seat of her truck.

"Damn, bitch, I been sitting here for three hours wondering when the fuck you was gonna wake up," Kendra said, while snacking on a bag of fruit snacks.

Looking around the parking lot of the restaurant, Storm rubbed the side of her head. "Why are we sitting here and what time is it?"

"It's six thirty in the afternoon and we've been sitting here for hours. Earlier, you said you felt dizzy. So I walked you to the car and Gotti's dumb ass showed up out of nowhere, like he was following us. He jumped out his car and asked can he talk to you. I was about to call the police on his ass, until you told me it was okay. After you guys talked, your ass climbed in the car and went to sleep. I been sitting right here like a lost kid at the damn aquarium. I thought yo ass was dead from how your mouth was hanging open." Kendra laughed.

"Oh my God. I knew I shouldn't have come here. Dominic warned me not to," Storm said, while searching for her cellphone.

"Warned you about what? I hope you're not referring that statement to me," Kendra spat.

"It's not about you, Ken. It's about me and my husband. I need to get home." Watching Storm crank up her vehicle, she stepped out with a look of hatred.

"I guess it's gonna be another year before I see you again, huh?"

I'm sorry," was her only reply before she pulled into the busy two-way street as her car blended in with the thick evening traffic.

Kendra pulled out her cellphone and dialed Gotti's number.

"What is it?"

"I don't think she remembers."

"Good, make your way back to me now. We need to talk."

Ending the call, she smiled before getting into her car. Plot one was down. Now she was about to sit and watch the rest unfold with ease.

* * *

Turning into the driveway of her home, Storm killed her ignition and stepped out of her truck. Trailing through the lawn, she made her way to the porch and removed her house keys. Walking inside, her feet collided with a bundle of suitcases.

"What the hell! Dominic, what is all of this piled up in front of the door?"

Making his way downstairs, he held Rain in his right arm. "It's all of your shit. The rest of it is in the hallway upstairs. I want you out of my shit by morning time."

"Excuse me?" Storm dropped her purse on the floor to meet him face-to-face.

"Oh, I'm sorry, let me say it in a way you can understand better. Get your shit, bitch, and get out of my house."

The strong language he used proved he was beyond serious. And the strong smell of Patrón liquor he was sipping on earlier lingered on his breath.

Standing with a shocked expression, Storm folded her arms. "Bitch? Dominic, what the hell is wrong with you?"

Smirking with a screwed face, Dominic pulled out his phone. "I guess you had a nice time searching for houses today, huh?"

Viewing the photos of Gotti on top of her, Storm snatched it from his hand. The sight of Kendra's evil smile spread through her vision as the tears began to fall.

"He raped me," Storm whispered. "Dominic, Kendra and Gotti are trying to set me up."

"Humph. Run that shit by a slow nigga. I guess she drugged you and pulled your pants down for that nigga to hit the pussy too, huh?"

Running a hand through her hair, she replayed the entire lunch back over with Kendra. Remembering the soda that caused her dizziness to start, she grabbed Dominic's shirt.

"Yes. Kendra did something to my drink. We were having lunch and talking. My head started to hurt—"

"And you lied. Why were you with this bitch? You told me that you were out looking for a new house."

"Because I thought she was my friend, Dominic. I would never cross that line with you ever again. You have to believe me. Look at me. Look at the damn pictures. I'm laying inside of a car with my eyes closed. Just look at it, baby. Please," she pleaded, while holding the phone up to his face.

Storm's eyes were pouring tears of the truth and Dominic could feel the sincerity in her tone. The confusion he felt at the time was starting to place a lock on his heart. Her past deceit weighed heavily in the current situation. So accepting that excuse off the bat was not in his plans. After studying the pictures for another minute, he placed the baby in her arms and headed for the door.

"Dominic, where are you going?"

"To see if your story adds up," he said, before walking out of the house.

Turning down Kendra's street, Dominic parked his car directly next to her Acura RDX. Climbing out of the driver's seat, he took two stairs at a time to quickly reach her front door. Giving two stern knocks, he could hear movements shuffling inside the apartment.

"I'm coming," Kendra spoke from the other side of the door. As she opened her door, Dominic shoved his Beretta in her face and pushed her inside. Kicking the door closed, he pushed her partially naked frame into the wall.

"Dominic, what the fuck are you doing?"

"I should be asking your sneaky ass the same thing. You running around with this nigga, Gotti, playing games after I warned y'all to stay the fuck away from my wife."

"Is that what she told you? That I'm helping him? I knew that you were a quiet person, but I never thought that you would be labeled dumb."

"What are you talking about?"

"That girl's playing your dumb ass like a five-year-old with a PlayStation on Christmas Day. You think some-body's forcing her to creep around with Gotti? That's been her nigga since they were teenagers. Are you really that slow? She's in love with him. If anything, I tried to warn you about her and you ignored every sign. Maybe you need to sit and have a drink to refresh your memory."

Taking a step back from him, Kendra fixed her thin nightgown and headed for the kitchen. Quickly returning, she placed a small glass in Dominic's hand before he sat on the couch.

"If what you're saying is true, why won't she just be with him?"

"Because you continue to forgive, you continue to love someone that has problems, but refuse to admit it."

Taking a sip of the drink, Dominic's mind flashed to Storm's situation and decided to pass on any beverages. Sitting beside him, Kendra looked into his eyes.

"You're being tricked, but it's up to you if that stops." The end of her words started to slur through his ears as if she was slowly drifting away. Dominic was so distraught about his problem, that Kendra couldn't tell if the drug was taking effect. Watching him stare into space, she slid a hand across his pants.

"I hate to see you suffering like this." After receiving nothing but silence, Kendra knew that he was finally vulnerable. Taking advantage, she placed her hand inside of his boxers. Removing his piece, she smiled.

"I just wanna help you, Dominic," she lied, before gobbling a mouth full. Feeling his member rise, she gagged and slightly closed her eyes. Dominic's body felt as if he were completely paralyzed. His mind said to choke the living hell out her, but his arms were looser than a bowl of noodles. Slobbing passionately on his piece, Kendra paused and stood to her feet. Dropping her gown to the floor, she straddled his lap.

"Get the fuck off me," he mumbled with sweat dripping down his forehead.

"Hold on, baby. It won't take long," she moaned, sliding down on his dick. "Sshittt!"

Placing one of her feet on the couch, Kendra bounced lightly, allowing him to fill her tight spot. As Dominic witnessed the devil take control of him, he silently prayed for strength. It was hard to believe a lot of Storm's accusations without any proof, but tonight clearly showed him different.

Just as Kendra felt herself about to cum, Dominic jolted his body forward, sending her to the floor. "Oh, my God. It's just how I imagined."

She snickered as Dominic tried to stand to his feet. Holding on to the wall for balance, he shook off the dizziness to look into her eyes.

"If you come anywhere near us again, I'm going to kill you."

"I'm counting on it, big daddy." Kendra spread her legs with a small laugh. Stumbling out of her home, he made his way down to the car. Forcing himself into the front seat, he dialed Storm's number on his car phone. "Hello? Dominic, where are you?"

"I believe you. I'm sorry. I'm on the way home," he panted.

"What happened? Are you okay?" she asked with worry.

"I'll be home soon," he said, before hanging up to catch his breath. The betrayal was beyond high and now it was clear that more than one person had a mission to fulfill.

Chapter 7

The next morning, Storm woke up in bed alone with a pounding headache and nausea. Tossing the cover back, she planted her feet firmly on the floor and rubbed her temple. Slowly getting up, she walked into the bathroom. Dominic was standing at the sink, brushing his teeth.

"Good morning."

"Morning," Dominic replied.

Storm raised the toilet seat and damn near stuck her head in it. A large amount of fluid poured from her mouth. Coughing violently, her body shook and broke out in a sweat. Dominic stepped closer to where she was slumped over.

"Are you okay?"

Shaking her head no, she continued to throw up and gag. Dropping to her knees, Storm covered her face, as she broke out in tears. "Dominic, I'm so sorry. This is all my fault. I should've listened to you. Now I've broken your trust all over again."

Kneeling down to help her up, Dominic grabbed her arms and pulled her from the floor. "Yes. You should've listened to me, but I told you last night I believe you."

"Are you sure?"

"Yes."

"Why do you believe me now? You were so adamant about putting me out."

Dominic hesitated, as last night replayed in his head. Kendra was truly a bitch on a mission and a hidden agenda. But, he didn't understand why she was hell bent on ruining his marriage with someone that was supposed to be her best friend.

"Contrary to your belief, I know when you are lying and telling the truth. I've studied you long enough to know the difference. Get yourself together. I'm headed to the dealership for a few hours."

Storm was still a little skeptical. She had gone through too much hell and high water to keep her husband, so she needed reassurance. Grabbing his arm, she tried to study his face.

"Are you sure we're okay? I don't want this to ruin us."

"I believe you, baby. I'll see you in a few hours."

"Okay." Ignoring the fact that her breath wasn't fresh, he kissed her on the cheek and walked out the bathroom.

Storm brushed her teeth, washed her face and hopped into the shower. As she covered her body with body wash, tears flowed down her face. Last night's events had her emotional. The one person she thought she could trust turned out to be a two-headed snake. The more she thought about the chain of events, everything started to come to light.

Storm finally came to the realization that Kendra was behind everything. Now she wondered if the day they bumped into each other was truly a coincidence, or if Kendra set that up and kept him in the loop of her where-abouts. The only question now was, why? Why was she was adamant in getting her and Gotti back together? Storm thought back to the day at the restaurant when Kendra suggested she sleep with Gotti and get it over with. Her response was clear as day as it played in her head.

'You got that right and I say if you want to fuck him, do it. Shit, I know I would. Just don't get sprung though,

because you know he gone fuck the air, shit and piss out your ass.'

"That dirty bitch," she mumbled, while turning off the shower.

Suddenly in a rush, she stepped out the shower and wrapped herself in a towel. Storm went to check on Rain. Satisfied that she was still sleeping, she got dressed and sent Tia a text.

Storm: Can you meet me now. It's urgent

Tia: Yes. Where?

Storm: Where are you?

Tia: Home

Storm: Omw

Tia: K

Storm dressed Rain, packed a bag and strapped her down in the baby seat. On her way out the door, she locked up the house and they were on their way. Tia was the last person she could trust at that point, or so she hoped. Soon enough, she would find out if she had at least one friend left. Thirty minutes later, she was standing on Tia's doorstep. As she waited to gain entrance, she kept her eyes towards the road. Gotti was known for following her, so she had to be aware of her surroundings.

Tia opened the door. "Hey, girl! Come in."

Storm stepped in and sat the baby seat down on the floor, while she sat on the sofa. Tia sat beside her and unstrapped Rain, freeing her. Kissing her chubby cheeks, she smiled. "Aww! Look at goddy's baby. I haven't seen you in a while."

"Yeah, you been missing in action," Storm replied.

"Girl, it's been crazy."

"What's been going on with you?" Storm sat back and crossed her legs.

"We'll get to that. What was so urgent with you?"

Storm closed her eyes and exhaled deeply. "Can I trust you?"

"You know that already."

"No. I mean, can I really trust you? Lately, I've been finding out people aren't who they appear to be. It's like the masks are finally falling off and I can see the evil now."

Tia sat the baby on her lap when she realized the conversation was about to get deep. "Storm, I've never crossed you."

Thinking briefly, she nodded her head before she replied, "I'm saying this because I don't trust Kendra."

"Why not?"

"When Jade committed suicide, she left a letter warning me to stay away from Kendra. She didn't go into detail about it, so I wasn't sure about what she meant. Then yesterday I met her for lunch and she drugged me so Gotti could rape me."

Tia's face was scrunched up and wrinkles appeared on her forehead. "Why would she do that?"

"She's helping Gotti. She took pictures of him having sex with me and sent them to Dominic. They're purposely trying to sabotage my marriage."

"Damn! That's crazy. Kendra needs her ass beat."

"Have you spoken to her?"

"Not since she dropped me off at the hospital. What did Dominic say about all of this?"

"He told me to stay away from her and I didn't. When I got home he had all my shit packed and sitting by the door. This is way more than I bargained for. I should've left Gotti where he was. I fucked up."

"Gotti needs his ass shot. I hope Dominic kills that bitch. You know he shot his cousin Clyde," Tia added.

"Yeah, I heard."

"How you know?"

"Kendra."

"Let me guess, she told you we dating too?"

"Yep! You already know."

Tia shook her head. "Well, it's deeper than that now."

"How so?"

"I'm pregnant."

Storm's eyes lit up. "Are you serious?"

"As a heart attack."

"Congratulations. I'm happy for you, even though I didn't know you was getting dick."

Tia bounced Rain in her arms. "I wasn't sure where we were going with it this time, so I didn't say nothing. But now that I know we're official, I can tell you."

"So how is Clyde?"

"He's doing better."

"That's good. Gotti is so nasty for that, but his day is coming. He might as well count his muthafuckin' days."

Tia's brow slanted slightly. "What are you going to do?"

"I'll think of something. He violated me and Jade. I owe him for that. He ruined my life."

"Hold up." Tia held her hand up. "What do you mean, he violated Jade?"

The guilt was still riding her mentally. In a way, she felt responsible for Jade's untimely demise. Had she not ignored her calls, maybe Jade would be alive today.

"Jade filed a police report." Storm became a little choked up. Pausing, she caught her breath and continued, "She was raped by Gotti."

"What?"

"That was my same reaction. I can't believe he would do something so foul like that."

"We talking about the same Gotti, right?" Tia scoffed.

"You know what I mean. Jade didn't deserve that and now I feel so bad. I have to do something."

"I have an idea."

"What?" Storm was curious.

"You'll see. Gotti and Kendra needs to be dealt with."

Tia went and picked up her phone from off the counter. Storm sat quietly as Tia spoke on the phone. It piqued Storm's interest, because she heard her say the address. Tia ended the call and sat back on the sofa.

"Who was that?" Storm was on high alert. True enough, she did trust her, but something wasn't sitting well in her spirit.

"You'll see when he gets here. In the meantime, what I need for you to do is get a restraining order on both Kendra and Gotti. At least this way, you will have it documented. That way you are covered and that will be considered self-defense."

"Okay."

Tia's telephone began to ring. She picked it up and looked at the screen. "It's Kendra."

"Answer it and see what she wants."

"Don't say anything." Tia slid the green icon and put it on speaker. "Hello."

"Well hey, girl. Long time no hear from."

"Hey."

"What you doing?" Kendra asked.

"Nothing. What's up?"

"Oh, I was calling to see what room Clyde was in. I wanted to come up there and see y'all."

Tia cut her eyes and mouthed to Storm, *this bitch.* Storm shook her head no, so she wouldn't disclose his location. "Oh, that's okay. He's not in the hospital anymore."

"Oh, he's out?"

Fed up, Tia snapped. "No, Kendra. He's in the damn morgue."

"Tia, I'm so sorry. I didn't know. Do you need anything? I can come by your house."

"No. That's okay. I'm not home."

"Oh."

"I just want to be alone. I'll talk to you later."

When Tia hung up the phone, Storm was looking at her sideways. Her brain was racked with confusion about the conversation.

"Why did you tell her he was in the morgue?"

"I don't trust that bitch either. If she's working with Gotti and he's the one that shot him, that might be a set-up. I'm not risking his life, because I'll kill Kendra's ass if something happens to Clyde."

"True."

There was a knock on the door. Tia and Storm looked at each other and remained silent. Handing the baby over, Tia went to the door and peeped through the hole. Opening the door, she stepped back and in walked a well-dressed man that Storm didn't recognize.

"Come in and have a seat, Detective. This is my best friend, Storm King. Storm this is Detective Saunders. He's the one working on Clyde's case."

"Hello," Storm said softly. She didn't know what was about to transpire from his visit, but if it would help get rid of Gotti and Kendra for good, she was a willing participant.

Chapter 8

Pulling into the car dealership, Dominic parked his car and quickly headed inside. Stepping through the front door, Jacob hopped up from his seat at the customer service desk.

"Dominic, what the hell is going on with you? Is everything okay? Man, we haven't heard from you in days."

Placing a hand on Jacob's shoulder, he thought before answering. Things were already getting far out of hand and exposing the recent drama would place everyone else on the edge.

"Everything is gonna be okay. There's a lot going on with a few personal things, so I may need you to step up and keep our affairs in order with the business."

"Dominic, I think we have a bigger problem than that," Jacob cut him off with a worried expression.

"What do you mean?"

Walking him towards the office, Jacob entered closing the door behind them. Pressing the voicemail button on the black business phone, Gotti's voice began to play through the speaker.

"Hey, fuck man. I'm guessing you told my baby mama to switch her number again, huh? You know, I learned something about you, old man. You don't like to accept the truth. You can't stand the fact of losing to me. I was being lenient at first, but now I see you don't respect the truth. I want my baby and that's not a request. If you feel I'm playing, I can give you something to prove that thought wrong. Everyone you love, care for and even the ones you barely converse with will die, if I don't receive my child in the next two weeks. I'm giving you an option," Gotti threatened before the message ended.

Rubbing a hand against his goatee, Dominic shook his head. It was never intended for the outsiders in their lives to be in the middle of Storm's poisonous escapade. Gotti was pushing buttons he didn't know existed and Dominic was devoted to ending his rampage forever.

"You don't have to worry about him. He just wanna be seen."

"Dominic, there's more. He left about ten messages. He threatened to kill everyone you're associated with. Don't you think that's something we should worry about? This guy nearly killed you in front of the dealership. Dominic, we need to call the police."

"That's what we not about to do. If you have forgotten, my background isn't too clean myself, Jacob. Getting them involved is like signing my own indictment. Have a little faith in me. I'm gonna handle this guy. Just focus on selling these cars." Dominic smiled, patting him on the back.

"You're right. You're absolutely right. If there's anything else you need, just let me know," he replied, while heading for the office door.

After Jacob exited the room, Dominic replayed Gotti's messages. The seriousness pumping through his tongue said things were seriously about to get critical. His words were infuriating, but Dominic refused to lay down by any means, especially when it involved the ones he cared about.

***

"Bitch, don't you think I know that? Why would you ask her over the phone about where Clyde is, knowing this bitch is the police? That wasn't in the plan, Kendra."

"Gotti, stop yelling in my fucking ear. I was just trying to help. Tia has no reason to feel like I'm doing anything sneaky. Her problem is with you, not me."

"Yeah and Storm is probably sitting down right now, giving her the scoop on both of us. You said she was acting weird and hung up. Does that sound like some shit Tia would do?" Gotti complained.

"So what the fuck should we do now, genius? Storm obviously knows, because she's not answering my calls. Dominic has her head wrapped tighter than bubblegum around a stick of glue. We running around in circles and nothing is happening."

"Maybe we wouldn't have to do this shit if you just tell me the fucking address."

"And I told you that's not about to fucking happen. If you kill him, I lose."

Before Gotti could reply, three loud knocks rang out against the front door. Looking over at Trel, who sat on the opposite couch, he hung up the phone in Kendra's face.

"Who the fuck is that?" Trel stood to his feet, walking towards the window. Peeping out the blinds, he turned around with wide eyes. "It's the fucking police."

Quickly grabbing his gun, Gotti jumped up and headed for the back door. Before he could open it, the sound of walkie talkies and dogs alerted him from the other side. Turning back towards Trel, he began to whisper. "If they ask you about me tell them you don't know anything. The last time you seen me was about two weeks ago." Gotti stressed before climbing up inside the hallway attic.

"I got you. I got you. Just stay put," Trel said, before the loud knocking erupted a second time.

Taking a deep breath, he moved to the front door and slowly opened it. "Uh, good evening, Officer. Is there a problem?"

Giving him a stern look, Detective Saunders stepped forward, clutching a white piece of paper in his hand.

"We're looking for Greg Daniels. I'm Detective Saunders with the Clayton County Police Department. This is a warrant for his arrest, so before I proceed with moving you out our way, I'll ask you one time. Is he here?"

"No, sir. I haven't seen him in almost two weeks."

"I'll be the judge of that." Saunders waved his hands towards the officers before pushing his way inside the trap spot.

"So I guess you don't know about the drugs that's being run out of this place either, right?

"Uh. No, sir. I've never been aware of that."

Saunders chuckled from his reply and continued to search the house top and bottom. After fifteen minutes, he approached Trel who was standing in the living room shaking harder than a leaf.

"Is there any other place you think Mr. Daniels would be at this time?"

Shifting his eyes back and forth towards the hallway, he swallowed his spit. "I-uh-haven't seen him. I don't keep in contact with him period."

"But he's your friend, correct?" Saunders asked, following his eyes to the hallway.

"Yes, but he's also a grown man that has his own life. I'm not obligated to keep up with him for any reason. With all due respect, all I can do is relay the message if I run across him."

Shifting his eyes up to the attic door, Saunders moved closer.

"I'm guessing it's nothing but old clothes and furniture up there, correct?"

"I'm not sure, sir. I've never been up there to find out."

Cracking a wry smile, Detective Saunders reached for the string and paused when the rookie officer entered the front door.

"Sir. The office sends word that the suspect is probably on the move elsewhere. The squad is ready to move out."

Glancing at Trel, Saunders passed him a small card. "Don't hesitate. I'll be close," he taunted before walking out the home.

Locking the door, Trel peeped out of the blinds before rushing to let Gotti from the attic. Coming down the small set of steps, he gripped his gun with anger flushing through his veins.

"What the fuck we supposed to do now? We gotta get the hell on, man."

Ignoring Trel, Gotti grabbed his small duffle. "First, we about to take care of those niggas, Clyde and Dominic. Then, I'ma pay this fuck-ass bitch, Storm, a visit."

He knew Storm was stupid, but he wasn't sure if she would play the cop games. At that time it didn't matter, because everyone who wasn't with it was surely against it. The games were done.

***

Storm walked out the courthouse feeling relieved. She had finally submitted the restraining order against Gotti.

That was her first step to freedom, but she had a feeling the small piece of paper would only enrage him more. Pushing the stroller, she made her way back inside the parking garage.

Unlocking the doors, she opened the truck door and strapped Rain down in her car seat. Folding the stroller, she tossed it in the trunk and proceeded to leave the lot. Halfway down the street, an incoming call from Dominic stopped the music.

"Hey, baby."

"Where are you?"

Storm contemplated on if she should tell him what she'd just done. "About to check out some houses."

"Cancel that and come to the dealership."

"Is everything okay?"

"Yes."

"I'm on my way."

"Okay."

Storm ended the call and jumped on the interstate. Thirty minutes later, she was walking through the doors of the dealership with Rain in her arms.

"Good afternoon, ma'am. How can I help you?" the receptionist asked.

"I'm here to see my husband, Dominic."

"Let me call him for you."

"He's expecting me."

"Okay. I still have to call him." She picked up the receiver and put it against her ear.

"Yeah," Dominic answered.

"Mr. King, your wife is here to see you."

"Send her back."

"Yes, sir. Go on back, Mrs. King."

"Thank you."

Storm walked briskly down the hallway and pushed the door open. Dominic had his back to the door, with his arms behind his back. When the door slammed behind her, he turned around.

"Hey, what's going on?"

"Have a seat. I have something I need you to hear."

"Okay," she replied nervously.

Storm sat down and crossed her legs in anticipation. Dominic hit a button on the phone, generating the message prompts. Then the message started to play.

"Hey, fuck man. I'm guessing you told my baby mama to switch her number again, huh? You know, I learned something about you, old man. You don't like to accept the truth. You can't stand the fact of losing to me. I was being lenient at first, but now I see you don't respect the truth. I want my baby and that's not a request. If you feel I'm playing, I can give you something to prove that thought wrong. Everyone you love, care for and even the ones you barely converse with will die, if I don't receive my child in the next two weeks. I'm giving you an option."

When the message came to an end, Dominic hung up the phone and sat down. Frustrated was an understatement. He was beyond that stage. Receiving threats was something he didn't take lightly.

"Do you have anything to say about what you just heard?" he questioned in a perpetually tired voice.

"I don't know what to say," she replied with a sense of quilt. "I know this is all my fault, but what am I supposed to do? Gotti has fallen into a downward spiral and hit rock bottom. There is nothing I can do to stop that."

"That's the wrong answer, love. This fool has left multiple messages about killing people close to me and the ones I love. Those threats include you too."

Storm placed Rain on her shoulder and rocked her. "What do you want me to do?"

"Absolutely nothing, love." Dominic allowed the sarcasm to slide off his tongue smoothly.

"Dominic, you wouldn't have called me here if you didn't want me to do anything," Storm stated with agitation in her voice. "Just tell me what you want."

"I want you to kill the attitude. I'm not the one that cheated with a fuckin' mental patient and had a baby. This is the mess you created for a few orgasms. I'm simply trying to clean up the mess."

"You're right." Biting her tongue wasn't what she wanted to do, but he was right. She inserted Gotti into their lives by spreading her legs, knowing damn well he wasn't stable.

Storm observed him carefully, as he reached into the desk drawer. Exposing his hand, he pulled out a small handgun and sat it on the desk. A huge lump formed in her throat as she kept her eyes trained on him.

"W-what is that for?"

"With everything that's going on, I need you to carry this for protection. I'm going to handle him, but just in case he sneaks up on you, I want you to aim it at his head and pull the trigger."

Storm nodded her head. Had she not heard the message Gotti left, she would've felt compelled to say no. The anger in his voice insinuated he was going to kill her and she needed to be careful.

Dominic tossed a pamphlet across the desk at her. "When you leave here, go to The Huntley on Park Avenue. Ask for a tour of the penthouse apartment and submit an application. Find out the move-in fees and then call me."

"What happened to us moving into a house? You changed your mind about that?"

"In the meantime, yes. At least until this shit with Gotti is over with. I'll feel better knowing you and my child are not alone when I'm not there. You'll be amongst tons of nosey neighbors and security."

"Okay."

"And another thing, do not tell anyone where we live. Not even Tia. The purpose in this move is to keep you undetected, got it?"

"Yes. I won't say anything. I promise."

Dominic walked over and took Rain from her arms. "Come on. Let me walk you out."

Storm left the dealership and headed straight to Buckhead. Even though Tia was on her side, she decided she'd take heed to Dominic's request. Looking down at the gun tucked securely in her purse, Storm prayed she wouldn't have to use it.

Destiny Skai & Chris Green

Chapter 9

Detective Saunders walked into the interrogation room and closed the door. Slamming the folder down, he pulled out the metal chair and sat down. The cat and mouse game with his fugitive was getting on his nerves and he was ready to haul his black ass in expeditiously. He had every intention on nailing that muthafucka to the cross.

"Comfortable, Ms. Mims?"

Toya crossed her arms, while rolling her eyes. She was pissed after she was escorted out of her home for questioning. "I will be when I can get out of here and go home."

"Well, that depends on how much information you can give me. So let's find out what you know."

"What are you talking about?"

A lot of hostility was in her voice since she didn't know the purpose of her visit. Saunders was slightly annoyed, so he cut right to the chase.

"What's your relationship to Clyde Daniels?"

"Listen, I don't know anything about what happened to him. So, I can't help you."

Frustrated, Saunders hit the table with his fist. "Be quiet and answer my questions. If you don't, I will haul your ass down to the county on some trumped charges that'll stick to your ass like that wig on your head."

Toya dismissed her attitude and started talking. "He was my boyfriend."

"That's better," he smirked devilishly. "And how long have you known him?"

"Five years."

"You said he was your boyfriend? Explain that to me."

"Last I checked we were together. We decided to take a break, but I didn't know he moved on."

"So did that make you angry?"

"No." she replied flatly.

"Are you sure about that?"

"Yes."

"The reason I ask is because you said." Saunders opened up the folder in front of him. "And I quote, 'You can stay here with that dead-ass nigga. He ain't gone make it no way.' You want to tell me what you mean by that?"

Those were the last words Toya was expecting to hear. Suddenly, she started to panic and stumble over her words. "I. Umm. I was upset that another woman was there. It caught me by surprise, because I knew nothing about this woman."

"Tia," he stated.

"I don't know her name," she lied.

"You sure about that?"

"Yes."

"What do you know about Clyde's cousin, Gotti?"

"I know he just got out of prison." The coldness of the room caused her rock back and forth, while rubbing her arms.

"That's it? You knew Clyde for five years and you know nothing about his cousin? I'm having a hard time believing that."

"I don't know him. All I can tell you is that Clyde didn't trust him. That's it."

"Now we're getting somewhere." He leaned back in the chair and crossed his arms. "Why didn't he trust him?"

"Clyde never told me. He just said that his cousin was getting out and he needed to keep him close so he can watch him."

"Where can I find Gotti? Seems to me you know more than you're leading me to believe."

"I don't know."

"Stop lying to me," Saunders screamed.

"I don't know." Her voice box rattled with nervousness.

"You wanna know what I think? I think Clyde dumped you for another woman. You became upset and plotted revenge with Gotti. You're the only one with a motive here."

Toya screamed back at him, "I told you everything I know. Why don't you go and ask Clyde, or bring in Gotti for that matter? You trying to pin something on me I had nothing to do with. I don't care where Clyde puts his dick. We not together anymore. And how do you know that bitch, Tia, didn't set him up? Asking me all these damn questions."

Saunders stood up and nodded his head. "How about I do that?"

"Can I go home now?"

"Of course you can't. Sit tight so I can have you booked in the county, smart mouth."

Detective Saunders left the room in a rush. He knew Toya didn't have anything to do with it, but he felt like she was still hiding additional information. Since that was his hunch, he decided to let her sit a little while longer, just in case she thought of something else.

***

Turning into the car dealership, Gotti flipped the switch on his headlights. Bringing the vehicle to a halt, he looked over at Trel in the passenger seat and frowned.

"That don't look like a confident face, my nigga. You sure you ready?"

Glancing at the entrance, he began to weigh his options. There was no such thing as talking Gotti out of anything he was guaranteed to do. His mind was lost and for the love of Storm, Trel knew he was willing to take on the entire world.

"To be honest, Gotti, I think this shit is stupid. There's no reason to take it this far. All we have to do is wait for the nigga Dominic, like you said the first time. Doing this will not bring her back to you."

"I'm doing it to state a message. Everybody take shit for a game, until a person you care for loses their life. The nice guy shit is what I tried the first time, or you must don't remember. I gave an option and a warning, but now there's no room for choices."

"There's always a choice, Gotti. Just because you're hurting doesn't mean everybody gotta suffer with you, big bro. This isn't about anyone else. It's about the girl. It's about acceptance. You have to accept she moved on and you two are over, Gotti. It's not anyone's fault but yours."

Gotti laughed before running a hand over his head in frustration. Sliding a bullet into his Glock 9mm, he pressed the barrel into Trel's jaw.

"You sound like you wanna make it my fault when I blow yo shit apart from yo body. I never seen a nigga who claimed to be about this life, but start to fold all because of a little blood being spilled. You were the same one on my bumper saying you wanted to collide with the movement. The same nigga I bust down every check with. Now get the fuck out the car."

Being a victim of his rampage was never the vision that Trel seen occurring. His defiance was strong enough to tear down everyone's life who was in a ten-mile radius. Gotti wanted victory of a slain situation and disagreeing at the time would obviously end with a hot bullet to the head.

Watching Gotti's chest heave with anticipation, he stepped out of the car, letting the cool night breeze caress his face. His watch read 10:30 p.m. and the traffic was little to none on the main road of Dominic's dealership. Hopping out of the car with a small assault rifle on his side, Gotti pointed it towards the entrance. Walking directly next to one another, they trailed through the parking lot until reaching the glass doors.

Taking his chances, Trel sprinted into action and brushed past Gotti, causing him to stumble. Dashing across the parking lot, he covered his head in fear. Gotti's mind said to kill him immediately, but the large space of vehicles made it nearly impossible. Leaving him to stand alone only meant one thing. The loyalty they shared was no longer there. Gotti made himself one promise. If Trel wasn't out of state by morning, everything around him would drop like a fly on a thousand degree sunny day.

Stepping through the front door, his eyes locked with Jacob and the female assistant standing at the front desk. "Where's the boss man?" Gotti shouted with venom spilling off his tongue.

Observing him lift the weapon to aim, Jacob grabbed his coworker and quickly hit the floor.

Standing across the street from the dealership, Trel could hear the bundle of gunshots being released inside the building. His heart was in pain for the innocent by-standers, but at the time, his life was more important. All he could think about was getting home to Chanel, so they could get out of Dodge from the maniac he once considered to be a friend. Pulling out his phone, he placed a call.

"Nine-one-one, this is Operator Jones. What is your emergency?" the woman asked.

"I heard numerous gunshots being let off inside of a dealership on Peachtree Street. I think someone may be hurt," Trel assumed, before hanging up the line and tossing the cellphone into the nearest trashcan. He headed in the opposite direction of the crime scene.

* * *

The loud banging on their front door caused Dominic to open his eyes and reach for the gun that rested on the nightstand.

"What was that?" Storm asked while holding his arm with a firm grip.

"I'm not sure. I think it was the door."

As Dominic climbed out of bed, the knocking began to grow louder. Cocking the hammer of his pistol, he whispered to Storm, "Grab the baby."

Dominic knew that only a selected amount of people were aware of their location, but for someone to be beating on the door of their home at one in the morning spelled trouble in capital letters.

Dispersing from the bedroom, Dominic crept down the steps and placed his eye to the peephole. The flashes of red and blue police lights danced through his pupils, causing him to open the door. Detective Juan stood with a serious expression and clenched his gun handle after spotting the weapon in Dominic's hand.

"There's no need to feel threatened, Detective. I'm licensed. Is there a problem?"

Storm crept down the steps with Rain snuggled in her arms. Walking up to his side, she locked eyes with Detective Juan.

"Dominic, what's going on?"

"I don't mean to wake you so early in the morning, King. But there's been a situation at your dealership. We might need you to come in for questioning."

Dominic's face screwed up from his statement. "Situation? What exactly are you saying? Was there a robbery or something?"

"I think we should speak on this matter in private. I'm not trying to alarm your family and wife, if you understand what I'm saying."

"Whatever you have to say can be said in front of me. This is my husband," Storm added.

She could feel the sorrowful aura pouring off his expression before he released the drastic words. "Your dealership was ambushed a few hours ago. There were three people killed inside that building and neither one of them was the shooter."

Dropping his head, his mind instantly flashed back to Gotti's devastating threat. Clenching his fist tightly, he took a step forward.

"Tell me this is a joke."

"I'm afraid not, King. I'll give you a second to get yourself together." Detective Juan confirmed.

Gazing back at Storm, he shook his head before moving past her to go to the master bedroom. Tossing on a pair of slacks and a t-shirt, he grabbed his cell.

"Do you think he did this?" Storm stood at the entrance of their room.

"What the hell do you think? You heard the messages, didn't you? It ain't no random goddamn shootings going on off Peachtree Street, Storm."

"But can you be sure he did this?"

"My coworker and employees are dead and you think we have to play a fucking guessing game to know your little boyfriend did this? I can guarantee he fucking did it!"

Stepping in front of him, light tears formed in her eyes. "I know that me apologizing can't bring anyone back and I also know you feel this problem happened because of me. I just want you to know and understand I will never go against you, Dominic. I stand behind whatever decision you choose to make."

His anger started to slowly subside after hearing the next remark escape her lips. "He needs to be taken care of. Please don't let him destroy our family. If he's hurting people you care about, that means he's hurting me. Please get rid of him. Immediately."

Kissing her hands, he gave a confident nod before heading back down to the officers that stood in their living room. Thinking a step ahead of Dominic, Storm grabbed her cellphone and began to plan further for their safety. If Gotti felt he was about to shed the blood of her family again, his plans were surely about to crash straight into a steel wall.

Chapter 10

The next day

Trel and Chanel were at the Hilton, laying low. After the incident with Gotti, he knew he couldn't stay at their place. So once he made it home, they packed up their things and checked into a hotel close to the hospital where she worked. If Chanel didn't have to submit an emergency leave, Trel would've left Atlanta hours ago. After the stunt he pulled on Gotti, he knew that his ex-boss would be looking for him. A shootout wasn't what he had in mind, nor was dying. He wasn't about to put Chanel in harm's way, so protecting her was his main priority. Therefore, Trel knew they had to get out of Dodge expeditiously.

"Bae, you need to hurry up so we can check out." Trel checked his phone and saw that it was a quarter to ten.

"I'm moving as fast as I can," she replied, while peeking from the bathroom.

When Chanel walked into the room, Trel was sitting on the bed, loading a gun. He had two guns in his possession. Standing up, he put one inside his backpack and the other on his hip.

"You really need both of those?" Chanel dropped her towel and rubbed lotion all over her smooth brown skin.

"You do know who I'm dealing with, right?"

"You're right," she agreed.

Chanel quickly put on her undergarments, a pair of jeans, tank top and some Tori Burch sandals. She could tell Trel was under a lot of pressure and suffering from paranoia, by the way he was fidgeting and watching the clock.

"We can go now."

Trel stood up and grabbed his bag. "You got everything?"

"Yes."

"You have all your paperwork?"

"Yes."

Chanel and Trel left the hotel in a hurry. Grady Hospital was less than ten minutes away, so it didn't take long for them to reach their destination. Gotti called him a few times last night, but of course, he didn't answer. The relationship they had was over, so there was no need in answering his calls or replying to his text message.

"Park inside the parking garage and I'll take the crosswalk." Chanel pointed him in the right direction.

"You sure?"

"Yes. It's faster this way. And besides, my nurse manager is waiting on me, so I won't be in there long."

"Good. I would hate to run into him with you around." Trel pulled up into the garage and pulled a ticket.

"He'll be pretty stupid if he comes here, especially knowing that the police are looking for him."

Trel dropped Chanel close to the crosswalk and stopped the car. I'll be parked close by, but call me so I can meet you right here."

"Okay."

Trel waited until Chanel was out of his sight to find a parking spot. Backing in, he placed the gun on his lap just to be on the safe side. He knew Gotti well enough to know if he got caught slipping, it wouldn't end well for him. As he waited impatiently, Trel took the Black & Mild out the ashtray and sparked it up. Taking a long drag like he was smoking weed, he filled his lungs and blew it out slowly.

A Dodge Charger with tinted windows drove by slowly, sending him on high alert. With his hand on his ratchet, he gripped the handle and took a deep breath. There was no telling what Gotti was rolling in at that point and he needed to be prepared. The car went to the opposite end and parked in the handicap spot. Relieved, Trel relaxed his hand, laid his head against the headrest and closed his eyes.

One hour had passed since Trel drifted off to sleep. He was taking a nap like he was scot free. The sound of two people arguing woke him up from his slumber. Trel jumped up and looked around, his heart was almost beating out of his chest. Glancing towards the opposite side of the garage, he witnessed Chanel arguing with a female. Throwing the car into drive, he rushed in her direction. Chanel and Toya came to blows before he could slam on brakes. Trel jumped out the car and grabbed the female Chanel was fighting. It was tough to get her loose, because she had a handful of his girl's hair. Trel grabbed the girl by the throat and squeezed it until she released her grip. Chanel managed to kick Toya in the stomach before Trel let her go.

Toya was livid, as she pulled away from Trel. "You pussy-ass ho. How you gone tell that detective I had something to do with that shit?"

"Fuck you, ho. I surely did." Chanel stood there in a fighting stance, just in case Toya ran back up on her. "You gone sneak me bitch and still get your ass beat."

Trel pushed Toya. "It's over with, so step. I'm trying not to put my hands on you." Then he turned to Chanel and pointed at her with a scowl on his face. "Get in the car."

As soon as Trel pivoted to the left Toya pulled out a switch blade and ran towards Chanel. "You gone be, right along wit' his ass, bitch."

On instinct, Trel pulled his ratchet from his pocket and fired a single shot into Toya's back. *Boc!* The silencer suppressed the sound of the gunshot. She fell forward and landed at Chanel's feet. Chanel stood there with a blank expression on her face.

"Get in the car. Get in the car," Trel shouted, as he hopped into the driver's seat.

Chanel hesitated as she watched Toya slither around on the ground. It was like she was frozen in time. Never in her life had she seen someone shot directly in front of her.

"Chanel, let's go." She jumped in the car and Trel hit the gas, flushing it down to the first floor. There was no doubt in his mind that they needed to get on the road and they needed to do it now.

***

Kendra paced the floor, biting her nails. "Why do you do shit like this? I told you to chill the fuck out and let me handle this. Not kill innocent people and bring heat on yourself."

Gotti eyes turned into venomous slits. Kendra was two seconds from getting slapped. "I warned that nigga about my seed and I'm tired of playing with these bitches. He needed to know my bite was bigger than my bark."

"Great job, smart ass. If you go back to prison, how the fuck you supposed to raise your child? I swear, you don't have the sense God gave a road lizard."

"I see you forgot who running shit," he snarled.

Gotti stood up and stepped close to her. Snatching her up by the collar of her robe, he put his face close to hers. Kendra could feel the air coming from his nostrils. "What I told you about your mouth? Didn't I slap you in it before?"

Kendra nodded her head up and down.

"Open your mouth when I talk to you."

"Yes." She nodded again.

"Ain't shit attractive about a bitch with a slick, nasty mouth, especially when you talking to a real nigga. Save that nastiness for when you suck my dick."

Kendra didn't flinch. She was actually turned on by his aggression. That was one of the things she liked about him. Kendra could feel his hand slide up her robe. Between her legs, moisture started to form as he palmed her booty.

"Stop worrying about what I'm doing. I got this under control. You understand me?"

"Yeah," she mumbled.

Gotti squeezed her jaw, then placed his lips on Kendra's mouth and kissed her aggressively. She kissed him back with no hesitation. Moving his hand, he used his fingers to part her lips and caress her clit. Kendra closed her eyes and raised her leg, giving him full access to her opening. Her breathing increased as their passion increased. Gotti lifted her up, walked over to the sofa and sat down. Kendra was now straddling him. She could feel his erection pushing hard against his jeans. Gotti unzipped his pants to give his wood some breathing room. Kendra grinded against him while sucking on his tongue. Gotti rubbed his dick against her lips and prepared for the plunge. Loud banging put an end to that. *Boom! Boom! Boom!*

"Go away," she screamed.

"It's Detective Saunders. Open the door."

"Oh shit." Kendra jumped up.

Gotti's eyes stretched wide as a dinner plate. He zipped up his pants and stood up. "Get rid of him," he whispered before going into the bedroom and closing door.

Kendra straightened herself up and opened the door. He was leaning against the frame like he had an attitude. "What?"

"Kendra Stokes?"

"Yes." She folded her arms. "What can I do for you?"

"I need to ask you a few questions."

"Now is not a good time."

Detective Saunders peeked inside. "Are you busy? It seems like you're relaxed."

Kendra wasn't feeling his attitude. "Yes, I am busy and if you must know, I was masturbating. But you interrupted that." She huffed and rolled her eyes.

Detective Saunders wasn't moved by her snappiness. Instead of going back and forward with her, he let himself in. "This won't take long."

"I didn't let you in though." Kendra slammed the door and sat down on the sofa. "Make it snappy before you get me out the mood."

Detective Saunders sat down once Kendra was seated. "I'm going to cut straight to the chase."

"Please do," she slickly stated.

"Where is Greg Daniels?"

"Who?"

"Don't play games with me. Where is your partner, Greg Daniels?"

"I'm sorry, but I don't know anybody by that name."

Detective Saunders reached inside his coat pocket and pulled out a photo. "This is Greg Daniels. He also goes by Gotti."

Kendra smirked. "Well, that's all you had to say the first time." She crossed her legs. "I don't know where he is. Nor is it any of my concern. He's not my man."

"That's not what I was told."

"So in other words, you believe in everything you hear?" She toyed with him.

"Listen, I can take you down to the station if you're not going to cooperate. I've had enough of your sarcasm. So, what's it going to be?"

Kendra knew testing his patience wouldn't help the situation, so she decided to tone it down for Gotti's sake. "I'm listening."

"We can start of by you telling me where I can find him." He propped his elbow up on the sofa.

"I don't know where he is. I haven't seen him lately and that's the truth."

"Weren't you with him the night you drugged Storm King?"

Kendra was not expecting to hear that and she almost panicked, but she had to remember was going to be a game of he said, she said. "Let me set the record straight on that, because I didn't drug anyone. Storm had too much to drink that night and ended up sleeping with her daughter's father. That had nothing to do with me."

His brow creased downward. "So you didn't drug her?"

"No. I have no reason to do that. Now, Storm on the other hand, does. She's a married woman running around with her ex-boyfriend and had a baby by him. If you ask me, she's looking for a way to save her marriage. I'm just a pawn."

Detective Saunders took out his notepad and pen and jotted down a few notes for his case. "Who is her husband?"

"Dominic King."

"Okay." He scribbled more notes onto his pad. "So, Greg Daniels did not rape the victim?"

"No."

"How can you be so sure?" The vibe he was getting from her wasn't a good one at all, but he didn't let her know that.

"They've been sleeping together for months. He doesn't need to rape her."

"Now, Ms. Stokes, are you in any way, shape or form, assisting Greg Daniels in any activity that he has going on?"

"No, I don't. I have no idea what you're referring to."

"Do you know his cousin, Clyde Daniels?"

"No."

Detective Saunders knew she was lying, but he hadn't put the entire puzzle together. After a little more investigating, he would have all the answers he was looking for. And if anything came back with her name on it, he was going to nail her to the cross. His job there was done in the meantime, so he stood up and pulled a card from his pocket.

"If you see him or think of anything further, please don't hesitate to give me a call."

"Will do, Detective. Have a good day."

"You too. Enjoy your session."

Kendra escorted him out the front door. "Oh, I plan on doing that."

Detective Saunders paused and looked her in the eyes. "So, if I run the security cameras back at the restaurant, I won't find you putting anything in her drink, right?"

"Not at all."

Gotti was sitting on the bed naked when Kendra walked in. She immediately dropped her robe and climbed on top of him. "Did you hear all of that?"

"Yeah. You did good."

"I told you I got you." She planted a single kiss to his lips. "Now all we have to do is take care of Storm once and for all."

"You need to give me the address and it's done." Kendra covered his mouth with hers to silence him. Then they picked up where they left off on the sofa.

Chapter 11

Arriving back from the U-Haul storage center, Storm pulled her car back in front of their home. Stepping out, she made her way inside. It felt unusual to look around their suburb street for trouble, but the recent event that took place the night before had everyone sitting on eggshells.

"Dominic?" Storm called out as she crossed the threshold.

Moving about through the quiet house, she checked his office and still received an empty room. Glancing out of the window, she spotted him sitting on the back porch. He was facing the opposite way, but Rain sat in his hands waving her arms back and forth.

Heading down the stairs, she made her way through the back door. Walking over to Dominic, she frowned after spotting the light tears that rolled down his cheek.

"Baby, are you okay?"

Looking into her eyes, he smiled. "I'm not even sure anymore, ya know? I'm starting to feel I made a mistake. Like I moved too fast."

Squatting down in front of him, she lifted his chin. "What do you mean by that? Made a mistake about what, love?"

Instead of answering, his head drifted off to the light blue sky and clouds that floated above them.

Scratching her forehead, she pondered on his remark. "Do you mean mistake as in marrying me, Dominic?"

Her words fell on deaf ears, he continued to rock Rain on his leg with an aggravated expression.

"Baby, I love you and I understand your pain right now because I just got over the same thing dealing with

Jade. I know you're furious, but it doesn't mean to stop fighting for our marriage and what we have."

"Why should I!" he shouted, causing her to jump. "I consistently gave you the world. My all. And you still devoured my heart into pieces. This man has come into my world and crashed it into the ground. I lost a friend who I've known for over fifteen years, a business partner. What the hell am I supposed to tell his family? His children?"

Listening to him vent, she could see the damage was taking effect on his emotions. Gotti was pushing every button he could to see his demise. Storm was his only connection left in the streets, besides his grandmother. After coming home and losing them, both made the true hate spill from his actions. It caused the animosity to grow bigger than anyone expected and the aftermath was now too much for him to handle.

"Ever since you decided to make me your wife, I knew my life would change forever. It was like a dream come true for me. I knew your heart stretched places where the average man couldn't reach. You were my king and I was your queen."

Laying Rain across his lap, he began to listen as her pain flushed out.

"I started to understand that more after you accepted me back for my mistakes. I knew your heart was golden, but I underestimated myself as a wife. I started to have doubts about being the one you accepted. I knew the pain I caused you formed deep scars that I would never be able to see heal. Sometimes I feel I don't deserve you because of the actions I took. Before I'll be with another man or let him win, I would rather for him to murder me in cold blood."

"That's not gonna happen, so don't speak like that. Yes, you did hurt me and sometimes it feels as if you didn't appreciate anything I have done for you. I married you because I was truly in love. Not because of what you have or the way you think. I knew the day I looked into your eyes I wanted to spend the rest of my days with you. Relationships are complicated, but disloyalty will only create a gap that will grow by the second, if you do things out of the boundaries of that relationship. We are family and family always strives and survives for each other."

The sound of a vehicle pulling into their driveway caused their conversation to pause. "Come in the house. Now," Dominic mouthed, before picking up Rain. Sliding through their back door, he adjusted the locks and handed the baby to Storm.

Hearing the doorbell sound three times, he grabbed his pistol off the living room table. "Go upstairs and close the door behind you," he ordered.

Following his orders, Storm made her way to the second floor of their home. Moving towards the front door, Dominic looked out of the peephole before opening it up.

"Dominic. I hope this isn't a bad time. I need a moment to have a conversation with you, if it's possible."

Clyde stood with his hands folded across his chest. The casual clothing he wore looked as if it came out of the latest high-end designer store. His face was calm and his posture would make you feel their current disaster never occurred.

Dominic began to clench his jaws before stepping outside in front of his former employee. "You got the nuts to actually step foot on my motherfucking property after all the grimy shit you brought upon my family? You must have a death wish, because if you ain't got my money, you might need to say a prayer for you to make it to the nearest hospital."

Smirking, Clyde pulled a cigarette from his collar shirt pocket. Placing a flame to the tip, he blew the tobacco smoke into Dominic's face. "I don't think the police would want you to do that. Detective Juan calls me every thirty minutes, just to make sure my safety is insured. Not to mention, the tracker that's on my cell. Rethink killing me on your front porch. Please."

Processing his words, he took a step back. "What the fuck are you doing at my home?" He kept the pistol in hand, just in case it was some sort of set-up.

"First, I just wanna address the fact that I'm even able to stand here in front of you right now. I mean, I was just literally laying on my death bed and by a small hair on the devil's ass. I was still able to see my friend Dominic."

"What the fuck do you want? I have no reason to be excited to see a nigga who crossed me."

"Define cross, Dominic? Because I think you've gotten shit confused on what occurred. Maybe we need to relapse for a second and go back. I brought this man into your operation to benefit you, motherfucker."

"I don't know what the fuck you're talking about. The only operation I have is a car dealership. And quite frankly, I'm not comfortable talking to rats."

Smiling, Clyde inhaled on his cancer stick. "Ya know something, bro? I tried to be loyal to you and I still ended up catching the terrible end of this. Gotti wasn't supposed to clash with you. It was supposed to be a movement for our business to grow and prosper. All I did the entire time of being around you was help. And where did that get me?"

Dominic stared him down with a menacing mug, as he continued to speak.

"See, the one thing you didn't ask yourself is did I actually set you up? Did I truly put a plot together to place you around this man? The one whose woman you decided to marry while he was incarcerated?"

"She's my wife regardless of who was in the past. Once I started my journey with her, it ended the road for him. That's life."

"Exactly. And at that time, life was running smooth. I've never even had the chance to meet the woman you both were fighting over. So instead of you idiots sitting down like two grown men, you clashed over pussy. A pussy that was obviously horny for more than one cock."

"I'll kill you where you stand, Clyde. Tread lightly."

"No. I think you need to tread softly, fuck man. Within a few weeks you're gonna have a case being placed against you for drug trafficking and I'm gonna be the state's witness. I'm gonna go in that courtroom and explain to everyone else what we were going through. Maybe I can receive a little closure that way, huh? See, Dominic, when you got a bunch of thirsty detectives ready to take down a mastermind operation, it causes them to do whatever to win. Even if that means to help another criminal, if you get my drift. The program I'm up under is witness protection management. They watch my every move twenty-four seven."

He nodded across the street to a parked black Mercedes. "It's okay, though. I don't have to wear wires. I don't have to record a conversation for evidence. I'm the only thing standing in your way to lose this trial and I'm willing to stand down under one condition," Clyde mentioned before tossing the butt of his cigarette.

"What the fuck do you want from me? Because I don't have anything for you. You're not welcome at my home and I think this little matter you speak on can be handled with a phone call to my lawyer."

"I'm afraid not, big guy. In the next few days, you'll be getting a warrant served to you for court. The only reason you haven't been picked up is because my mouth hasn't given anything valuable to snatch your ass out of this home at a thousand miles an hour. So, with that being said, it's time to switch up on the game plan a bit. You pressured me to get your money and now the tables have turned. I want four hundred thousand dollars delivered to me for the troubles and I'll be out of your hair. We wouldn't want Detective Juan to get involved with getting any statements from me before their investigation is done now, would we?" Clyde said, straightening out his sleeves.

"You're not gonna win. Slimy bastards like you never will."

"That's the trick, Dominic. We are all entitled to feel the way we do. Especially when it comes to extortion or let's say, blackmailing. You have two weeks to get the money to me or Stormy will be fucking more than an ex after the feds raid your house and ship you both to opposite sides of the earth. Have a good day, Bossman." He laughed before walking back to his car.

Watching him pull out of the parking lot, Dominic stepped back inside to Storm standing at the bottom of their staircase. "Baby, who was that?"

Looking around with a nervous posture, he opened his mouth to speak. "We have to move. Tonight."

Chapter 12

One week had passed since Storm and Dominic moved into their new place at The Huntley on Park Avenue. The penthouse suite was absolutely stunning, but she preferred a house. Dominic promised it was only temporary and a way to ensure she and Rain were safe during his absence. Once he took care of Gotti and he was out the way, then they could move.

Storm sat on the bed and watched Dominic get dressed in his street gear to go to the dealership. Trepidation settled heavy on her heart, as she thought of the possibility of him not coming home.

"Do you really have to go?"

"Yes. I have a few things I need to do. It will only take a few hours. It's not like the dealership is open."

"That's more of a reason for you to not go." Storm did her best to fight back the tears, but the truth was, she was afraid Gotti would kill him. Their last encounter landed Dominic in the hospital. She knew this time bullets were going to fly and she couldn't risk him going inside of a body bag.

"Please don't go," she pleaded.

Dominic tucked his gun into the waistband of his jeans and stood in front of her. Wiping the lone tear from her eye, he kissed her forehead. "I promise I'll be back. Just relax. Nothing is going to happen to me."

Storm nodded her head, but she wasn't one hundred percent sure about his promise. "You promise?"

"Yes. I promise."

Storm walked Dominic to the door and kissed him on the lips. Her embrace was tighter than usual. "I love you, Dominic. Please come back to us."

"I will."

Dominic walked out the door and she immediately checked the clock. It was noon. Therefore, she was expecting him back by three o'clock.

Rain was sound asleep, so she fixed herself a cocktail and retreated to the balcony to enjoy the view of the Atlanta Skyline. The baby monitor was nearby just in case she woke up hollering. In her glass was mango pineapple Svedka, mixed with orange juice.

Thoughts of Gotti flashed through her mind, causing her to shudder in fear. Everything that was going on in her life was her fault. If she would've kept her distance, none of this would be happening. Storm took another sip of her drink.

"How could I be so stupid?" she mumbled.

Gotti was once the man that she loved and adored, but he quickly turned into someone she hated with a passion, the man she wanted dead. If that was the only way to get him out of their lives, then it had to be done. He had to go. There was no way she was willing to lose Dominic behind the bullshit she created.

Storm's phone started to ring and her heart dropped to the pit of her stomach. Fumbling her drink, it almost slipped from her fingertips, but she caught it and sat it on the patio table. Quickly, she snatched the phone up.

"Hello."

"So, these the kind of games you wanna play, bitch?" Kendra spat.

"Who the fuck you think you called?" she questioned, while staring at her phone screen. To her it was obvious that Kendra had the wrong number.

"I know who I called. I'm talking to the police-ass hoe that told them folks, I drugged her and let Gotti rape her."

"Kendra, you did drug me. I'm far from stupid."

"No, bitch. You're closer than you think." Kendra was livid and high out her mind. "You running around making false accusations, knowing damn well Gotti don't have to rape you. He can fuck you anytime."

"Listen, don't call my phone with the bullshit. I don't have time for your drama. You know what the fuck you did."

"I'm not Jade! You can't shut me up or tell me what to do. I'm not scared of you."

"You heard what the fuck I said." Storm was now standing on her feet. She was furious at the way Kendra was coming at her. "Now, keep on trying me."

"So, what you saying? You wanna fight?"

"Kendra, you don't want these hands. I promise you, sis."

"As a matter of fact, I do. Just wait on it, bitch. I'm gone teach you about playing with me."

"This is so funny to me. How in the fuck can you be mad at me for something you did to me? I'm the one that should be mad. You drugged me and let him rape me. Then you sent pictures to my husband's phone. That's some foul shit."

"You had it all and you ruined it. Don't get mad at me, because you can't control the urges of your pussy. You wanted to fuck that man since day-one. So don't blame me for your fuck-ups."

Storm wanted to beat Kendra's ass. If she didn't have Rain with her, she would've pulled up on that ass. "Bitch, you the same one I confided in. You told me to do it and get it over with."

"That was once and I was drunk. Nobody told you to keep fucking him and have a baby from his ass. That was on you." Kendra sat down on the sofa and got comfortable. She was pissed, but her voice was calm. "I will say this though. I can see why you couldn't stop fucking him."

Storm couldn't believe what she was hearing.

"You don't deserve Dominic and I don't understand why you keep dragging him along, when you in love with your child's father. Just run off and be a family with Gotti, so I can get him out my hair. Aren't you tired of hiding from him?"

Rain's cries flooded the baby monitor, taking her attention from Kendra. She pulled the patio door and proceeded inside. "Fuck you, Kendra, and don't call my phone anymore. Whatever you and Gotti are trying to do isn't going to work. I'm never leaving my husband and you can tell him that."

"Oh, I'll be seeing you real soon, bitch. So you better walk light." Kendra ended the call and tossed the phone beside her on the sofa.

***

Tia was at home, lying down with Clyde, watching the reality show, *Love after Lockup*. They felt comfortable within their living quarters, since they had an on-duty cop outside of their home for protection.

Clyde rolled over on his side and placed his hand on his growing seed. "One more week and I'll have enough money for us to skip town. We can get the hell up out of here and start a new life."

"Where are you getting the money from? You haven't been working," Tia questioned.

"Don't worry about that. I have everything under control, believe that."

Tia wasn't feeling his response, given the chain of events he recently went through with his cousin. She didn't want him to get back into that lifestyle again. Clyde needed to be around and help raise their child.

Grabbing his face, she looked deep into his soul for the deception that lay in his eyes. "Tell me the truth. You've kept me in the dark for far too long and that's not fair to me. If I'm going to up and relocate with you, you need to be honest with me. You need to tell me everything you're involved in."

Clyde closed his eyes and exhaled. Tia was right. There was no one in his corner except her. He knew he could trust her and of course, she had his best interest at heart. Slowly, he opened his eyes and exhaled once more, before giving her the rundown on his plan. Tia sat quietly, while he shed light on things she had no knowledge of.

Once he was done explaining, he replaced her thoughts with two powerful orgasms. That easily stopped her from asking any additional questions. Tia laid in bed attempting to fall asleep, but the sandman was nowhere near. The heavy knock on the door startled her. Clyde was gone to handle some business, which meant she was without security. Whoever who was knocking was impatient, they knocked harder. Tia jumped up from the bed and grabbed her .380 handgun from her nightstand drawer.

"If this is Gotti, I'm shooting his ass today." Tia walked slowly down the hall with her hand at her side.

As she peeked through the peephole, she recognized the face and tucked her gun underneath the sofa cushion. Disengaging the locks, she opened the door.

"Detective Saunders, how can I help you?"

Before he could respond, his partner answered the question for her. "Katia Johnson, you are under arrest for assault with a deadly weapon. Anything you say, can and will be used against you in the court of law."

Tia was flabbergasted at the accusations he was making. "What are you talking about? I didn't assault anyone."

The detective grabbed Tia forcefully by her wrists and slapped the cuffs on, while continuing to read her, her rights. Detective Saunders finally spoke up. "Easy man, she's pregnant. Tia, just relax and we'll get to the bottom of this."

"I didn't do anything," Tia cried, as she was being escorted to the squad car. "I need to call my boyfriend."

Her pleas went unheard. Thirty minutes later, she was at the Atlanta Police Department, sitting inside the interrogation room. It was cold and all she had on were a pair of sweats and a tank top. Tia wanted to cry because she had no way of contacting Clyde to tell him where she was. His cell number was not registered into her memory bank.

A few minutes passed before a female officer came in and had a seat. "Katia Johnson?"

"Yes."

"Do you know why you're here?"

"No I don't."

"You're here for your involvement in the shooting of Latoya Watts."

"Who?" Tia was confused.

"I see we need to refresh your memory about the woman you had the altercation at the hospital with."

Tia thought for a second and that was when she realized they were talking about Toya, Clyde's ex-girlfriend.

Chapter 13

Future's hit single, *Honest,* pumped through Gotti's hotel speakers, as he tossed back three more X-pills. Ever since the dealership shooting, he decided to keep a low profile for a very short moment. The hit made every big news station and the last thing he needed was his name being mentioned over the airwave. His facial hair was beginning to sprout and the aggravation over the Storm situation was eating at his anger by the hour.

Lifting the liquor bottle to his lips, he glanced at his cellphone. Kendra's name danced across the screen twice before he decided to pick up. "Where the fuck are you? You know I need some pussy on these fucking pills, Kendra!"

"Nigga, I'm pulling in the fucking driveway downstairs. Stop yelling at me. You need to be focused on what we been speaking on these past few days. This bitch is starting to get beside herself."

"What the fuck did I tell you about the way we talk on these phones now? There was no need to call me if you were making your way up the damn stairs."

Hanging up the line, he tossed it back on the table. Sparking his marijuana, he began to nod his head to the music. His moment of peace quickly ended when she barged through his hotel door.

"You didn't have to hang up in my face. Just because you feel we aren't in any committed relationship, doesn't mean you have to treat me like a fucking prostitute."

Kendra's neck was crooked and a disgusted look was plastered across her face.

"Shut up before I slap that stupid smirk off yo face. If you haven't noticed, you're the only one yelling right now," Gotti spat before turning the music off. "What the fuck is your problem?"

"Storm. The bitch is spitting a mean bark through the phone and I think it's gonna be a problem because we just had words. I asked that bitch if she wanted to fight and she started to do all this animated shit."

Shaking his head with a pathetic look, he brushed off her statement.

"First of all, you're not about to do shit to my bitch. The only thing you're supposed to be doing is keeping her in the chokehold with the calm conversation. I'm not trying to make these bitches aware that I'm coming slow ass girl. That's the reason I been sweating in a hotel for a straight week. All you have to do is follow the plan."

"And what's the plan Gotti because it switch every damn day. You wanna kidnap this girl. Then you wanna kill Dominic, which is not about to happen. What gives you the bright idea that he's just gonna let you kill him, huh? He's waiting for you to pull some slick shit Gotti. You beat this man unconscious in front of his business. I think that I would be prepared for you to. Especially when you just fucked her and sent the evidence to this man's phone. You need to listen to me and we'll both leave from this situation satisfied."

Smiling, Gotti folded his arms. "I guess we should just let you take over the whole mission too shouldn't we? I mean you shouldn't mind killing a motherfucker if I came down to it. Because this shit get deeper than that big ass mouth you be running. Dominic is lost. I got mind control over Debo. He don't know whether I'll come while he's sleep or if I'll show up while they're having a fake ass family brunch in the nearest mall. You see I'ma man with great vision."

Gotti boasted before hitting his blunt. "He's hiding because the wolf is on the loose. It's only a matter of time before it all crashes to an end."

"Yeah, but what'll happen when your little queen wants to alert the authorities. I'll tell you something that you might didn't know about your filthy Pocahontas. She will snitch under pressure. You're gonna wait so long to handle this that by the time you find her and Rain, a group of federal agents will be finding you. That bitch is scared. She's gonna tell."

Standing up, Gotti stretched his arms. "I guess it's that time of the day huh?"

"What the hell are you talking about?"

Before she could get out another word, he slammed a forceful open hand across her jaw. "Didn't I tell you to start fixing the way you talk bitch."

"Okay Gotti, I'm sorry." Kendra was in the fetal position beneath him.

Picking up the remote he resumed the music to block out any ear hustlers. "Take this shit the fuck off. Get up!" He barked, ripping her thin sweats in two. Grabbing her by the hair, he bent her over the small suede couch.

"Gotti, please!"

Ignoring her cries, he grabbed his bottle to use the liquor as a lubricant. Pouring the liquid down her round shaped behind, he jammed his rod inside her womanhood.

"Ahhhhh!"

Gripping a handful of ass, his hard thrust began to turn into deep slow strokes. The resistance in Kendra's body started to loosen and her muscles began to flow along with his rhythm.

"Didn't I tell you not to act like that?" He asked before dipping into her belly.

"Yesss!" she grunted with pleasure. Licking her luscious lips, she began to twirl her clitoris in a fast motion.

It was sad to say, but the force of Gotti's dick placed a deep spell over her mind. It was forbidden to date a man with an intoxicating sex game. The rules constantly were broken when it came down to a sweaty and sticky orgasm. Feeling her hypnotic backside collide with his piece, he placed a hard open hand down on her right ass cheek.

"Make that shit cream for me." he teased, while placing a finger in her butt.

"Okayyy!" she moaned before arching her back higher.

After a full session of makeup sex, Kendra laid next to Gotti as he flicked through his cellphone messages.

"You know that these cops are riding around looking for you right?"

"Nah Kendra. I didn't have a clue. Of course I know. That's the reason I'm putting the rest of my shit on pause. I'm gathering up my dough. Then I'm snatching Storm and Rain up and I'm out of this bitch for good."

Sitting up with the blanket covering her breast, Kendra stared into his eyes. "What do you see in her so much? I mean, why fight so hard for someone that doesn't want to be saved."

Sitting back, he pondered on her question. The love he shared for Storm wasn't a package that could be purchased from the corner store. It was embedded from the day they met.

"After these next few days. It won't even matter." He mumbled before sliding back on top of her.

***

Sitting at the desk in his private office, Detective Juan did a complete history search on Gotti's criminal record. The information he was receiving changed the total outlook on the way he viewed his suspect. It was tough chasing a person that cause problems for the citizens of the city. But Gotti was the type who wouldn't stop until a gun and a bullet were involved. All of his charges since a teen involved a weapon or lead to a victim being shot numerous of times. It was obvious the man they were looking for wasn't going out willingly.

"So what's this about?" Saunders walked through the door of his office.

"It's about this case. The guy we've been searching so hard to locate. Have you done the background on this guy?"

"Of course. The streets are talking Juan. He's a menace. The hiding game can only last for so long. Your victim is friends with my suspect's little girlfriend. It's clear that someone isn't being honest here."

"That I understand. I'm speaking on his history with firearms. This guy has an ass of aggravated assaults. He's dangerous."

"And so is the police department of this state."

"You're missing my point Saunders. The dealership shooting that occurred last week. This fits his description."

"What gives you that bright idea?"

"Because he's screwing the owner's wife."

"What?"

"Clyde Daniels and Greg Daniels are cousins. Dominic King is married to Storm King. The same woman who's on Greg Daniel's emergency calls list inside the institution."

Standing up, he stared at the computer. "Well I'll be damned. Maybe she's working with him?"

Shaking his head, Detective Juan sat back in his chair. "It's bigger than that. I think we're looking at a love triangle here. She's not helping him. She's running away from him."

"If he has anything to do with this, everyone who's involved with this guy is going down. Is this what you wanted to tell me? That the suspect is having a fling with this guy's wife. The same guy that you've been chasing for the past ten years about drugs. Detective Juan, I think you're getting off track here." Saunders stated with a hint of aggravation.

"You're wrong. I think I'm on the correct track. You're missing the grand picture that's in your face. Clyde Daniels is affiliated with Dominic King. So is Greg Daniels."

"Clyde Daniels isn't your problem Juan. He's mine. While you're sitting in here chasing a false stash spot, I'll be cracking this case and sending this asshole to prison forever. See you at the finish line Detective."

"You're gonna get someone killed. These people have a deeper problem than you see. If you alert the problem with force it may cost someone's life in the end. These aren't ordinary criminals we're dealing with."

Smirking, Saunders opened the office door. "Too bad that I'm no ordinary detective. Sorry that we can't say the same for you."

Watching him slam the door and leave the station, Juan switched his eyes back to the old mugshot of Dominic that sat on his laptop.

"What do you have going on now Mr. King?" He mumbled.

Lifting his office phone, he dialed the front desk secretary. "Yes Detective?"

"Cindy, if it's possible could you get in contact with my suspect's parole lawyer and grab all of his recent addresses."

"Right away, sir."

"Cancel all my plans today. I'm heading out to check on a few things." He mentioned before grabbing his overcoat.

Something big was about to occur and he was gonna be sure to interfere and get to the bottom of it. The vision of Gotti continued to run through his brain. It was easy to read the eyes of a hurt man. He just prayed that his pain wouldn't lead to any more deaths.

Chapter 14

Tia was booked into Fulton County Jail with a seventy-five-thousand-dollar bond, dressed down in county blues and escorted to a dorm. Due to the fact that she didn't know Clyde's number by heart, she couldn't call him to post her bond. That only left Storm to come to her rescue, but she didn't get an answer when she called from the free phone. Not once in Tia's life had she been to jail. Needless to say, she was nervous as hell. It wasn't that she couldn't hold her own. The situation was just awkward and crazy at the same time. Not to mention, something she had no parts of.

As she walked inside the dorm, she was thrown off by the amount of noise coming from the women. There was a lot of laughter going on, card games being played and rap battles. The only thing she wanted to do was sleep her time away until she was able to walk back out those doors. Tia walked past a few rooms with her things in tow, until she was approached by a female with short, curly hair.

"There's an empty bunk in my room. You can take it if you like."

"Sure."

"Follow me. I'm Stacy."

"I'm Tia." Tia followed Stacy into her room where she was shown her bunk.

"You can get right up there." Stacy grabbed the semi-raggedy mattress and tossed it on the top bunk.

"Thanks." Tia rubbed her arms, as chill bumps made themselves present.

"No problem. This your first time locked up, huh?"

Tia grinned. "It's that obvious, huh?"

"You're more nervous than a whore in church." Tia couldn't help but to laugh. "See, that's it. Loosen up. It's not that bad, unless you gone be in here for a long time."

Tia became tense just thinking about it. Although she had a bond, she didn't want to think there was a possibility that she would have to do time in the end. True enough she was innocent, but that wouldn't be the first time someone was locked up for a crime they didn't commit.

"I hope not," she replied.

"What did you do?" Stacy asked.

"That's the thing. I didn't do anything."

Stacy nodded her head. "Yeah. It's innocent until proven guilty. I can dig it."

"Seriously, I didn't do anything. They arrested me without evidence."

Stacy put her foot on the bottom bunk and leaned against the metal. "So what did they arrest you for?"

"Aggravated assault."

"Oh, you beat somebody ass," Stacy giggled.

"No. It's my boyfriend's ex-girlfriend. She's lying on me."

"Damn." Stacy rubbed her forehead. "That's fucked up. Have you been to first appearance court yet?"

"No."

"What's your bond amount?"

"Seventy-five thousand."

"That's a lot to pay. You have someone to get you out?"

"Not yet. I can't remember my boyfriend's number and my best friend didn't answer the phone when I called."

Stacy thought for a second. Then she sat down on the bed. "Sit." Tia did as she was told and took a seat on the cushioned bunk. "Okay, so when you go to first appearance court, you need to ask for a bond reduction. It's your first time in trouble, so they should grant it for you."

"I appreciate this, because I have no clue about what's going on with me or what I need to be doing."

"No sweat. I'm about to go out there for a few. Get comfy and relax a little."

"Okay."

Tia fixed up the makeshift bed and laid down. All she could do was stare at the ceiling and try her best not to cry. A few hours later Tia was called out for first appearance court. Her knees buckled as she waited to see the presiding judge on the monitor. As fate allowed it, the person in front of her was a friend of the family and her bond was reduced to twenty-five thousand dollars. Tia was extremely happy when she returned back to the dorm. The first stop she made was to the phone to call Storm. As the phone rang, she rocked her leg impatiently.

"Please pick up. Please pick up." Then finally, her prayers were answered. The recording played it itself out, seconds later her call was accepted.

"Tia!" Storm screeched. "What are you doing in jail?"

"It's a long story, but I'll explain it to you later. In the meantime, can you please come and bond me out?"

Storm walked out the bedroom to make sure Dominic couldn't hear her. "How much is it?"

"Twenty-five thousand, but with a bondsman it will be four thousand. I'll pay you back. I promise."

"Okay. I can come in the morning when Dominic leaves. He's not going to let me leave the house at this hour."

"That's fine. I just need to get out of here. They have me in here on these bogus ass charges, but I'm going to get an attorney to help me out with this. I can't go down for something I didn't do."

"It's killing me not knowing what happened, but I can wait. How are you? Nobody's tried you, have they?"

"No. I'm good. My bunkmate is cool, so I'm good."

Tia and Storm talked until the fifteen minutes ran out and the recorder warned them. "You have one minute left."

"Well, that's the end of the call. I'm about to lay down and sleep until they call my name for release."

"Just hang tight. I'm going early in the morning. So you should be out by noon."

"Thanks, Storm."

"You're welcome."

"I love you," Tia added.

"I love you too. Keep them legs closed in there."

They both shared a laugh before the call was disconnected. Tia went back into the room and wrapped herself up in the state issued blanket and closed her eyes.

***

Storm was up at seven in the morning to prepare for her day. To her surprise, Dominic was still asleep. Rubbing his shoulders, she whispered in his ear. "Dominic, wake up."

He stirred around in his sleep, but he didn't move. Storm figured he was tired, being that he didn't go to bed until two in the morning. However, she attempted to wake him up again. "Dominic, baby, you not going to the dealership today?"

Dominic squinted his eyes and yawned. "What?"

"It's seven o'clock. Are you going to get up and get dressed?"

"No. I'm not going in today. It's not ready to be opened up just yet."

"Okay. Well I need to run a few errands. It won't take long. I'm going to put Rain in the bed with you, okay?"

Storm knew that was her chance to escape without the questions, so she threw on a pair of jeans, a tee shirt and some sandals. Rain was knocked out in her crib, so she picked her up gently and prayed she didn't wake up before she left. Dominic was lying on his back when she returned.

"Babe, here she goes."

Dominic turned on his side. "Lay her right here." Storm laid Rain right up under Dominic, kissed his forehead and rushed out the door.

Storm left the high rise building and hopped onto Peachtree Road NE, en route to Big Daddy Bonds near Gotti's grandma's house. Storm was happy the parking lot was empty when she got there. As expected, Phil was sitting behind the counter, twisting a blunt.

"That's what we do now, smoke in front of our customers?"

Phil stopped mid-lick to see who was trying to check him. A wide smile crept across his lips as he stood up and stepped from around the counter. "Well, I'll be damned. If it ain't goddamn Storm."

She smiled and gave him a hug. "Yes. It's me."

Phil was a big burly dude, that stood at six foot three and weighing every bit of two hundred seventy-five pounds. He was mainly muscle, because of football.

"What the hell brought you by here? I know damn well Gotti not locked up again."

"If he is, he can stay there."

"Oh, y'all done broke up for good this time?"

"Yes, we have."

"That's crazy. I saw him a few weeks ago and he told me y'all were married and just had a baby."

Storm wanted to correct the lies Gotti was spreading, but decided against it. "Yes, we have a little girl together, but that part of my life is in the past."

"Hey, I don't blame you." Phil leaned against the counter and folded his arms across your chest. "So, what can I do for you?"

"A friend of mine is locked up at the Fulton County Jail and I need to get her out."

"What's her name?"

"Katia Johnson."

"A'ight. Give a minute."

Phil walked back behind the counter and sat down at his desk, while Storm kept looking out the window. The last thing she wanted was to run into Gotti on his side of the tracks. A few minutes later, Phil was back at the counter.

"Okay, so her bond is twenty-five grand. With me, it will be four thousand to get her out. Are you paying cash, using collateral or both?"

"Cash. Well, check actually."

Phil smirked with a bit of disappointment. "I normally don't take checks, but since I know you, I'm going to make an exception."

Storm pulled out her checkbook. "Well, I appreciate that, because I don't carry cash and I don't want to go to the bank. The money is there. Don't worry."

"I know your face clean. You been using me for years with Gotti's crazy ass. His ass better stay out this time. He should be tired by now."

"We'll see about that." She smiled.

Storm filled out the necessary paperwork and left the building. A little before noon, she received a call from Tia, letting her know she'd been released. Tia was standing at the entrance when Storm pulled in. She jumped inside the truck and sighed heavily.

"Thank you so much for saving me. Girl, shit is crazy."

"I can see that. What happened?"

Tia gave Storm a complete run-down on what led to her arrest, including the details about her and Toya's altercation at the hospital. As Storm listened, she made her way back to Phil, so Tia could fill out her portion of the forms.

"They feel like you guilty already."

"Tell me about it. I just need a good attorney to help me get out this shit."

"That you do."

Storm and Tia walked inside the bails bonds shop and stood at the counter. "Phil," Storm called out. "She's ready to sign."

The sound of Storm's cell erupted inside her purse, getting her attention. When she pulled it, she walked outside to talk in private. She wasn't trying to raise any suspicions as to her whereabouts.

"Hey, my love. Are you awake now?"

"Yeah. Where are you?"

"I just had to run a few errands. I'll be back shortly."

"Well hurry back."

"I'm about to leave the store now."

"Okay."

Storm ended the call, grateful that she didn't have to lie about her location. Upon re-entering the building, Phil was handing Tia some papers. "When the case is over, you can get your money back."

"Thanks, Phil," Storm said sweetly.

"Anytime. Take care of that baby."

"I will."

On the way to the car, Tia handed Storm a copy of one of the papers. When she looked down at them, she realized her new address was on there. Storm hoped that Tia wasn't paying attention to the information. It's not that she didn't trust her friend, but she couldn't afford to breech her security or safety. They climbed into the truck and Storm pulled off.

Chapter 15

It was bright and early in the morning when Detective Juan's phone vibrated on top of his kitchen counter. Sitting down the coffee mug plastered to his fingertips, he picked up.

"This is Juan."

"Detective?"

Hearing Trel's voice, he quickly dashed towards his office to retrieve his recorder. "Mr. Williams. How are you? I'm glad you were able to call."

"Yeah. I know I really didn't have a choice. So I'm just ready to get this over with to make sure my name is cleared."

"And I totally understand your reasoning, son. It's not easy to give your life for the mistakes of another being. But, we choose to do the best we can, in order to survive for the next trial and tribulation."

"Tell him about the shooting with Toya. It will clear us," Chanel whispered into his ear. Shooing her away from the cellphone, he stood up to make his away across the room.

"Yeah. You're right. It's not easy. But at the same time, it ain't hard. I have nothing to do with this guy's actions, so what all does this requires me to do, because I ain't testifying on this man for nothing."

"Well, we're sitting back with three different bodies on our hands, from the man who you're not willing to testify against. These individual's families deserve justice. I mean, Mr. Williams, have some compassion for Christ's sake," Juan stated before leaning against his kitchen table.

"Let me inform you on something, Detective. This isn't one of your little fairytale cases that's gonna get you a promotion from a witness. This isn't what I do. I'm only complying for the cause of my woman. The first thing you need to understand is that man ain't nothing to be fucked around with. He's dangerous. The only thing he cares about is that girl. I mean, after he lost his grand-mother, he ain't been the same. Storm was the only thing keeping him balanced and he had that taken away also."

Clearing his throat, Detective Juan quickly reached for pen and paper. "Did you say Storm? Do you mean Storm King?" he questioned, already knowing the answer.

"I guess. I'm not a part of the family. I just know that whatever she did to him, he's obsessed with this woman. It's deeper than I can understand."

"And what about the dealership?"

"I think you already know all that I have knowledge of."

"I'm looking for the motive, Williams. You helped a man make a bad choice and you actually had the chance to call someone to help those people. It's more to this story, but you're not being a team player in order to put this case on a death bed."

"What do you want from me, man? I told you what I knew, that's what we agreed on, remember?"

"No, what we agreed to was you helping to put this animal behind the walls for the rest of his life. If you're not trying to be a part of that, I would suggest you find a great suit and get ready to explain this story for twelve others."

Taking a deep breath, Trel placed the phone on mute. "He wants me to testify on Gotti."

"I don't give a fuck. That bastard gotta get what he deserves. He tried to kill us, Trel. Handle this so it can be done. I'm not gonna be able to rest until I know he's gone for good," Chanel said with her arms crossed.

The rules in the game were simple. We all could play with fire until it was time for you to get burned. Gotti was making things hotter than usual and a bid was out of the question for Chanel. It was sad to handle the situation so sloppily, but at the time it was either family, or the fake love from a nigga who claimed to be a friend.

Placing the phone back to his ear, he gave in. "I'll do it."

"Good. I'll be in touch," Detective Juan assured before hanging up.

Calling the superior court judge of Cobb County, he had the warrants signed to either bring Gotti in by surrender or death. It was officially about to be a manhunt.

Grabbing his keys, he left his home and headed straight for the police station. Dialing a number on his cell, he touched the speaker button.

"Detective Saunders speaking."

"Saunders, I need you to do a search unit for me. The suspect needs to be on the public enemy list."

"You know we aren't allowed to do that without a judge's signature."

"I'm on my way to the station. It's already being faxed over."

"Well, I'll be damned. I guess I can come out of retirement now," Saunders stated with a chuckle.

"Yeah. Just one thing."

"What's that?"

"Please don't kill him. There's justice that has to be served for these families. Let them receive that."

"I'll do my best," he replied before ending the call.

* * *

Swerving out of his local weed man's trap spot, Gotti did the dash towards the mall West End. His bloodshot eyes were an indication that he'd been smoking his time away. The nervousness had yet to subside. Storm had literally disappeared and the feeling of his baby being held away from him only caused more anger.

Calling Kendra, he turned the music down so he was able to hear.

"Hello?"

"Where are you?" Gotti questioned.

"Nigga, I'm in the same spot you left me. You could at least bring me something to eat, since I'm not allowed to leave."

"What the fuck did I tell you about your mouth? You must want that ass beat."

"Maybe." Kendra smirked with her fingers on the inside of her sweats.

"I'm asking where you are in the room."

"The front area."

"Go to the guest room on the other side and look under the bed."

Standing to her feet, Kendra made her way through the side door. Heading towards the bed, she flipped the mattress and found two chrome 9mm pistols.

"Where the hell did these come from?" Kendra asked through the receiver.

"Don't worry about all that. Grab it and make sure it's loaded."

Checking both clips, Kendra placed them back into the handle slot. "It looks good to me."

"And the bag up under the bed?"

Getting on her knees, she reached under the frame and pulled out a black Gucci duffle. Unzipping the bag, her eyes grew large from viewing the rolled rubber bands of cash. Thumbing through a knot, Kendra quickly estimated about twelve grand.

"Where did you get all of this bread?"

"Don't worry about it. All you need to know is I'm trying to see what you wanna do. I got plenty more where that came from."

"What do you mean, what I wanna do?" Kendra was a little puzzled.

"About leaving. I been thinking—"

"About what?" she asked out of turn.

"Damn, bitch, can I speak? Shit. Now like I was saying, I been thinking about starting our own little thing. It ain't like Storm trying to be with me. I just want my daughter and I'm good. We can take the paper and just build a new life, ya feel me. What you think about that?"

Laughing out loud, Kendra smacked her teeth. "Gotti be for real. You don't want me, boy. I mean, it sounds good, but what do me and you really have in common? We were once friends. Now we're fucking each other and trying to set my best friend and her husband up for a death wish."

"Listen, shawty. I have nothing else but my word and my actions. Plus, we ain't just been fucking. We been having bare-dick freaky sex. Ain't no way you think that pussy going anywhere. You belong to me now, Kendra."

Flashing a devilish smile, she placed a hand on her hip. "So you in love with this, huh?"

"Don't get beside yourself. Let me come back and get drunk before you start kicking that word right there."

"Bye, nigga. Hurry up and get yo ass back."

"Now look who's talking. Sounds like you the one in love." Gotti laughed before hanging up.

Before he could turn his music back up, the sound of police sirens flooded his ears. Reaching for his gun that rested in between the car seat, he glanced in the rearview and spotted two police cruisers on his tail. Not wanting to make more of a scene to alert backup, he began to slow down his vehicle. Coming to a halt, Gotti placed his foot on the brakes, but didn't kill the ignition.

Watching the men step out of their cruisers, he knew it was a chance that he couldn't waste time with. Jumping from the driver's seat, Gotti began to let his gun bark loudly.

Boc! Boc! Boc! Boc! Boc! Boc! Boc! Boc!

Watching one of the officers fall to the concrete, Gotti jumped back in the car and put the pedal to the floor. The tires of his Charger burned a circle across the ground, before he skated off through the red light.

"I'm not going back. I'm not going back!" he yelled to himself. Bending a few corners, he made his way towards the expressway for a quick getaway.

Chapter 16

Tia pulled up in Clyde's driveway, only to find him sitting on the porch talking to a female. Putting the car in park and killing the ignition, she jumped out and rushed towards them. They glanced in her direction, but continued with their conversation. That made her blood boil. Tia walked up and stood in between them.

"You see me standing here." She mugged Clyde hard.

"How can I not? You only standing in my face," he replied casually.

"Excuse us. We are talking." The girl rolled her eyes.

Tia turned towards the female and put her hand in her face. "I don't give a fuck. This conversation is over." That was when she realized it was Toya's friend from the hospital. Tia turned back to Clyde.

"So you sitting out here talking to this bitch friend? The same one I had beef with in the hospital?"

Toya's friend rocked on her heels. "Girl, you better be lucky you pregnant, 'cause you talking real reckless right now."

"Don't let that stop you," Tia shot back.

Clyde stood up just in time to catch Tia's arm before she popped off, and push her down in his seat. "Chill out. It ain't like that." He then turned his attention back to the friend. "Thanks for stopping by to let me know what's going on, but you gotta go."

"Just make sure you go and check on my friend." She then walked off and pulled out her phone.

"Yo, what the fuck was all of that? You know that wasn't necessary."

"I don't give a fuck. You don't need to be talking to her, period. That's the same bitch that was in the hospital capping."

Clyde knew that was a no-win conversation. Wiping his hand across his forehead to catch the sweat, he sighed. "She only came by to tell me about Toya."

"Oh, you mean the fact that I got arrested for some shit I didn't do?"

"If you want out of this situation, you need to chill out. All that yelling and poppin' off ain't gone get you nowhere, but back in a cold-ass cell."

Tia thought about what he said and closed her mouth. Folding her arms across her chest, she rocked back and forth in the metal chair. "Fine. I'm calm."

"Good. Now, like I was saying, she wants me to come by her house to see her."

"For what?"

"I don't know, but that's the only way you're going to get these charges dropped, so I have to do it. She knows you didn't do it, but this is her way of getting you back."

"Okay, so when we going over there?" Tia hissed.

"How is that going to look if I bring you with me? You need to think about what you saying. I don't want that girl, so you don't have to worry about that." Clyde stood in front of her and grabbed her hand. "I'm only doing this for you. If you wasn't caught up in the mix, I wouldn't even be going."

"I hate to say this, but go ahead. I'll be here when you get back."

Clyde planted a kiss on Tia's lips before he jogged down the walkway and up to the unmarked police car.

Forty-five minutes later Clyde was knocking on the door of Toya's apartment. The door opened and as expected Toya's friend was staring him in the face.

"I see you made it."

Clyde walked past her. "Yeah. Where is she?"

"In her room."

Clyde walked down the hall and entered the bedroom to find Toya reading the book, *True Savage* by Chris Green. He sat down beside her. "How are you?"

"I'm okay."

"That's good. So, what did you want to see me about?"

Toya closed the book and placed it beside her. Toya's eyes met his and locked in. "You do know all of this is your fault?"

Clyde's brow raised. "How? I had nothing to do with this."

"Oh really?" Toya rolled her neck. "How, Sway? Let's see. You tell me we need to take a break, but come to find out you have a new bitch and a baby on the way. You could've handled me way different than that."

Toya's eyes began to water, because she did love Clyde and he hurt her deeply. Using the back of her hand, she wiped her eyes. "That was so foul on your behalf. I'm thinking we were going to get back together, but meanwhile you out here starting a family and shit. And look how I had to find out."

Clyde sat in silence trying to find the correct response. "Toya, it was never my intention to hurt you and I want to sincerely apologize to you. We haven't been happy together in a long time, so you knew there was a chance we wouldn't get back together. The relationship I have with Tia just happened out the blue. We used to deal with each other back in the day and when I ran into her, we just rekindled that old flame. This had nothing to do with you."

"That's not how it felt, but okay."

"Okay what? You accept my apology?"

"I guess I don't have a choice."

Clyde pondered on his next thought before he said it. As bad as he didn't want to bring it up, he didn't have a choice. "Does that mean you're going to drop the charges? You know she didn't do that."

Toya rolled her eyes. "You don't know that."

"She's not capable of doing that. So, yes, I do know that."

Playing with her fingers, she stopped and looked up. Her dry tears stained her face. "Do you love her?"

"I do," he replied with no hesitation.

All she could do was nod her head up and down. "I respect that and I will call the detective tomorrow and let him know she had nothing to do with it."

"Seriously?"

"Yes. All I wanted was an apology. You have my word. I'm not going to get in the way of your happiness. Thanks for stopping by to check on me." She stated genuinely.

"You're welcome and thanks."

As much as she hated what happened between them, she couldn't make Tia suffer for something Clyde did to her. He owed her communication, not Tia. And for that reason, she felt it was best to let go while she still had her dignity. Toya watched Clyde, as he walked out of her room and out her life for good.

***

Storm was lying in bed peacefully when she felt someone push her legs open. Between motherhood and moving into the new place, she was always tired. Sex between her and Dominic was long overdue, so she just laid there and let him take the lead. The brush of his fingertips across her nipples summoned a moan. Then she felt him palm her breast through her silk nightgown. Gently, he nibbled on her earlobe, as his hands roamed up her silky, smooth thighs.

"Mm," she hummed with her eyes still closed.

Storm's body was now on airplane mode and she was ready for his next move. Slowly his hands moved upward and rested on the base of her neck. The grip was soft at first, but then it grew tighter instantly and she could feel a shortness of breath. Suddenly, her eyes opened and the body that towered over her wasn't Dominic. It was Gotti.

Storm grabbed his hands and tried to free herself, but he wasn't letting up. Scratching and clawing, she did her best to get him off of her to no avail. However, she didn't give up. Wildly, she swung her arms, clunking him in the face. Finally, she was able to scream.

"Gotti, please don't kill me!" she shouted at the top of her lungs.

"Storm! Storm! Wake up." Dominic shook her from the nightmare she was having.

When Storm finally opened her eyes, she was sweating profusely. Her heart was thumping hard through her chest. Looking around the dark room, she reached for the lamp in order to see his face. Dominic's eyes were red and barely open.

"It was just a dream. You okay?" He placed his hand on top of hers.

Storm still seemed discombobulated. "I'm going to die. I can feel it, Dominic."

Dominic sat up in the bed and pulled her close to him. "You're not going to die. I'm not letting that happen."

"I am. He's going to kill me."

"Trust me. You'll be safe. I promise." Dominic shook his head because Storm made it seem like he couldn't protect her. After a few moments, he put his pride to the side and decided she felt that way because Gotti could defeat her.

"Where's the gun I gave you?" he asked.

"In the drawer."

"I'm taking you to the gun range tomorrow. I need to be sure you can shoot, just in case you run into him when I'm not around."

"Okay." Storm cuddled up underneath Dominic and closed her eyes. He, in turn, rocked her in his arms until she fell asleep.

The following day, Dominic and Storm dropped Rain off to a daycare owned by a female friend of Dominic. Of course she was reluctant to do so, but Wendy assured her that Rain was in good hands. Storm was able to relax once she realized they could watch Rain on the daycare app. Wendy downloaded it to her phone and eased her anxiety. Once Storm saw her baby on her phone, they were able to head out.

Dominic took Storm to the gun range on Bishop Street. Once inside, they stepped to the counter and greeted the associate. "Good afternoon, is Matt here?" Dominic asked.

"Yes. He's here. Can I tell him who's asking?"

"Dominic King."

The clerk walked away from the counter and into a back room. Approximately two minutes later, she reappeared with Matt on her heels. Matt was a biker-looking dude with a long, salt and pepper beard.

"Dominic King." He smiled as he walked up and shook his hand. "It's good to see you, my brother."

"Likewise, brother. This is my wife, Storm." They greeted one another, one by one.

"What can I do for you?" Matt placed both hands on his lips.

"My wife is a beginner and she needs to get some practice in."

Matt nodded his head up and down. "That won't be a problem, but I do suggest that she takes the thirty-minute safety orientation first. It would be better for her. I'll even throw in two hours of range time for you."

"I'm paying you for everything."

"Nonsense. You've done a lot for me."

"I won't have it any other way." Dominic reached into his wallet and handed over three, crispy one-hundred-dollar bills. "Waive the thirty-minute orientation."

"No problem. Let me get y'all situated."

Matt set them up in the range and went back to work. Dominic and Storm put on the goggles and ear protection. Walking up to the booth, he picked up the Colt .45 and fired a few rounds. Storm jumped every time a shot rang out. When he was finished, he changed the target practice paper and showed it to her.

"You see that bullseye? That's where you want to aim. Head and chest shots. Your assailant is guaranteed to die if you shoot properly."

"Okay."

"Step inside the booth, baby."

Dominic stood behind Storm and guided her trembling hands. "Why you shaking? Don't be nervous. Just remember you have to protect you and Rain. Once your defense mechanism kicks in and your adrenaline is rushing, that fear will go out the window."

"Got it."

Dominic held her wrists to make sure the gun didn't kick back and she lost control. The last thing he needed was a fatality. The first two rounds were the toughest ones, but by the third go-round she had improved tremendously. Two hours later, Storm was shooting like a professional. Dominic took down her practice paper and handed it to her.

"Nice head and chest shots. You think you ready?"

Storm was satisfied with the progress she made, along with the comfort of pulling that trigger. Before that, she was certain she wouldn't be able to shoot Gotti, if need be. But she never disclosed that information to Dominic. After the lesson, she was confident she could protect herself and her baby.

"I'm ready."

"So, if he tries to kidnap you, where are you going to shoot him?"

"Head or chest."

"Good. Let's go and get our baby girl. I'm sure she misses us."

Dominic and Storm left the range and headed back to the daycare to retrieve Rain.

Chapter 17

"The bastard shot at me. He literally jumped out of the car and shot at me," the rookie officer said with fear lacing his tone.

"Wait, slow down, all you have to do is tell me exactly what happened," Detective Juan said with a calm voice.

"The suspect we were on the lookout for. We found him. I had his picture in the center of my dashboard and he stopped at a red light directly next to me. I followed him down the street for a while to make sure I had a positive identification. After I was sure, I hit my sirens."

"And?"

"He slowed down and got out with a gun in hand. Before I could pull my weapon, he started to let off an ass of shots at us. All I could do was take cover. He caught me off guard. It was like he knew we were coming for him," the officer replied honestly.

Detective Juan couldn't take the pressure behind what was next to come for the force. There was now an officer laying in the intensive care unit at Grady Memorial Hospital, because of Greg Daniels. The feds were bound to sweep in for an answer at any time and the solution was going be one that ended up with the entire department working at the nearest gas station or food mart.

Swerving up to the scene, Saunders stepped out of his car and headed straight through the caution tape. His suit jacket was off and the sleeves of his collar shirt were rolled up to his elbows. Walking with a stride as if he were on a mission, he stepped in front of Detective Juan.

"So, I'm guessing you have this part of the story figured out too. Right, Juan?"

"No, but I'm working on it now. It's going to be handled and truly, nothing is normal about this. That officer had no authority to go after Daniels on his own. Protocol specifically said to call the higher ranks if this guy was spotted, so the blame is placed on him."

"No! No fucking way. You expect to catch a masked murderer without thin chances, Juan. He's a criminal. When did we have to start calling anyone to catch a bad guy? Please let me know. I have an officer sitting in the infirmary right now with two gunshots to his neck and face. I want this motherfucker dead!"

"Well, I'm afraid the police force just don't kill people Detective Saunders." Juan was now standing in his face with a bold stare. "I don't know if you're forgetting your job description, or if you're just on a rampage for blood, but intentions matter in this department. We can't handle this problem with reckless emotions."

"I gave my life to this department twenty years ago. I'm one of the best detectives on this force."

"And if you want to remain one, you'll calm yourself and act accordingly. I'm doing all I can to make sure this guy is brought down. He's not coming in easily. But we're the ones who's going to put this corruption to rest."

"Just to make things clear, Juan. This isn't your case alone and you also have rules that you're going to abide by as well, unless you want to be back behind a desk," Saunders threatened before walking off through the crime scene.

* * *

Moving around the hotel room, Gotti grabbed all of the things that would leave any trace of them being inside of the building. After rounding up the clothes and money, he made his way back into the front room where Kendra stood with her eyes glued to the screen of a television.

"This is news reporter, Edwin James, for the Fox news station. Right now, it's two o'clock pm and I'm deep in the Cobb County area with the police force standing right behind me. This is the scene where a wanted criminal held a vicious shootout with authorities, leaving one in critical condition and two more with minor injuries. The suspect is labeled to be highly dangerous." He mentioned, flashing a mugshot of Gotti on the screen.

Cutting her eyes at him, Kendra stepped into his face. "You shot a fucking cop. Gotti what's wrong with you? These people are gonna be looking everywhere for you. What the hell were you thinking?" she yelled with her hands moving around like a soccer goalie.

Ignoring her, he continued to listen.

"Right now, I'm going to have a word with the lead detective on the case about this issue and see if he can specify a few more things."

Detective Juan's face appeared on the screen seconds later. "As of right now, we're being very precautious with this individual. He's extremely dangerous and his mind isn't correct right now. The Cobb County police force has this under control and we will make sure this matter is taken care of immediately. Mr. Daniels is considered a menace to society and if you see this man, you are to go the other way and alert the authorities. Please call Crime Stoppers."

Cutting off the television, he continued to bag up their clothes.

"Gotti? Where does this leave me at? I can't run around

with you if these people are trying to kill you. How could you be so stupid?"

Rushing towards her, he wrapped both his hands around her throat. "Why can't you just shut the fuck up? Huh? You ain't going nowhere, bitch. I don't give a damn if the president was looking for me," he barked, while slightly shaking her. "All you have to do is let me run the show. Do you understand?"

Trying her best to breathe, Kendra still managed to nod her head in a fast pace. Letting her go, he pulled one of the chrome pistols from his waist and placed it into her hand.

"From now on, we move everywhere together. I'm gonna make sure I protect you by any means necessary. The police aren't my problem, because within the next three days, we will be sippin' coconut martinis on a beach. All we have to do is snatch Rain and handle the last of this business."

"Why can't we just leave now and never come back?" Kendra asked with tears in her eyes.

"Because it don't just work like that. Storm has my seed and I'm afraid that nigga Dominic has to die for the disrespect. They brought this on themselves. Nothing is more foul than the shit she pulled on me. We don't have compassion for them because those are just the ins and outs of this sick twisted game."

Kissing her lips softly, he wiped the tears from her face. "We need to get out of here. It's time to handle this but what are we going to do now?"

"We finna take a trip to Tia's crib" he replied before they exited the hotel room.

* * *

Pulling down Tia's street, Gotti parked his car eight houses down and climbed out. Waving for Kendra to follow him, she stepped out looking from side to side.

"Listen. All you have to do is get the bitch to open the door. After that. I'm gonna handle it all from there."

"I don't know about this, Gotti. What if Clyde tries to attack me or some shit? I can't beat no nigga."

"If that nigga touch you, I'ma blow his shit on Tia's mantel piece. I'm gonna be on the side of her house. Trust me," Gotti said, before cutting through the back of a neighbor's yard.

Strolling her way down the block, Kendra walked into the yard and knocked twice. It didn't take long for Tia to crack the door with the security chain still attached.

"Kendra. What are you doing here?"

"Damn bitch. You got me standing out here like I'm a damn stranger. What's wrong with you?"

"Uh. It's not like that, Ken, but there's a lot being said in the streets right now."

"Excuse me? What does that mean?"

"I mean everyone is saying you're not right."

Before Tia could finish her sentence, Gotti climbed over the porch banister and kicked the door in.

"Get up, bitch," he barked while towering over her.

Shaking away the dizziness from her vision, Tia began to slowly crawl backwards. "Kendra. What is he doing here? Please just leave."

"I'm afraid that's not gonna happen." Bending down, Gotti looked into her eyes and smirked. "Where is he?"

"Who?"

"My fucking cousin. Stop playing with me."

"He's not here. We have nothing to do with you guys issue. Please Gotti don't hurt me!" Tia begged.

"I'm not. If you don't make me of course."

Tia cursed herself for leaving her gun inside of the bedroom. Clyde warned her that Gotti was very slick. His mind was lost and there was no sense of direction in his brain. It was hard to believe that she wouldn't lose her life before he departed, so a closed mouth was her only option.

"So when is the last time you talked to Storm? I heard they moved. You wouldn't happen to know how to get there would you?" Gotti's eyes told a story that couldn't be understood. He was the definition of a true maniac.

"I haven't talked to Storm. Ever since y'all started having problems, she's been distant. You're ruining her life, Gotti. What do you expect?" Tia said truthfully.

"Girl, Storm is filling your head with bullshit. She's playing you. I bet you didn't know that her and Dominic was trying to have Clyde killed about that large debt he owe either, huh?"

"What debt? What are you talking about? Clyde doesn't owe Dominic anything and Storm would never be a part of something like that."

"How do you figure?" Gotti asked before walking over to the purse that sat on the living room couch.

"Because she's my friend."

"Right." Dumping out the contents inside her bag, Gotti grabbed her cellphone and scrolled through the recent calls and messages. There was no luck, because all he found was Storm's old cellular number. Picking up the folded piece of paper that blended with the pile, he spotted the bail bondsman title on top. Reading for a second, Gotti glanced over to her. "I thought you haven't spoken to Storm?"

"I haven't, I swear," Tia replied.

"Then why did she just bond you out?" he countered with a wicked smile.

Feeling her heart collapse, Tia stumbled over her words. The bond paper completely slipped her mind. Not to mention, Storm's signature was directly on the front in black ink. Spotting the address, Gotti slid the paper in his pocket.

"I think you need to keep this between us, Tia. You're my friend, but you're blind. It's either Storm or your child's father. You have to make a choice," Kendra spoke with folded arms.

"Oh, she's gonna keep it quiet, because you're coming with us," Gotti said, before placing Tia in a strong choke-hold. Struggling to get free, her legs kicked violently as she felt her body start to grow weak. Clawing at Gotti's arms, the sight of Kendra standing in front of her began to fade before she blacked out completely.

Chapter 18

Kendra managed to get away from Gotti for a little while, so she decided to do a little detective work without him. Before getting started, she made a pit stop by her house and then made her way to the liquor store. As she sat in the car, she took a shot of Patrón, straight out the bottle. Digging inside her purse, she pulled out her happy tube and snorted a small pile of cocaine. Squeezing the bridge of her nose, she closed her eyes and cleared her throat.

"I'm on your ass, bitch," Kendra spat before blasting Beyoncé's song, "Ring The Alarm" and speeding out of the parking lot into oncoming traffic.

Following the GPS for the next twenty-five minutes, she ended up at The Huntley on Park Avenue. Lowering the volume, she drove through slowly and backed into the furthest parking spot, away from the entrance to keep from being seen. "Hmm. So, this is where he's hiding you at," she mumbled.

Getting comfortable, Kendra fixed her a cup and watched the door in hopes that Dominic or Storm would surface. That would be all the confirmation she needed. Thirty minutes later, her phone chimed, shaking her corrupted thoughts. Glancing at the screen, she saw that it was Gotti.

"Shit!" she screeched. As bad as Kendra wanted to ignore it, she knew that wouldn't be wise. So she picked up. "Hello."

"Where you at?"

Kendra needed to come up with the quickest lie possible. "I'm about to pick up some food. Do you want something?"

"Where you going?"

"My favorite soul food spot."

"Call me when you get there, so I can tell you what I want."

"Okay."

Kendra hung up and tossed the phone in the passenger seat. When she looked up, her eyes zoomed in on the male figure leaving the building. For a split second she thought it was Dominic, but she was wrong.

As time continued to pass, she realized she had been sitting there for more than an hour. Kendra was tired of waiting and decided to up her crazy just a bit. Picking her phone up, she googled a number and dialed it.

"The Huntley on Park Avenue. This is Alyssa speaking, how can I help you?"

"Yes, hi. I'm interested in viewing one of your apartments. How do I go about scheduling a tour of the property?"

"I can assist you with that. What's your name?"

"Melissa Dunn."

"And how many bedrooms are you interested in?"

"One."

"Okay. Go to our website and you can request a tour online. We also have a virtual tour on that site as well, if you're interested in doing that."

"Umm. Yeah. No. I'm not interested in doing that. I would prefer to see with my own two eyes, what my money will be paying for. That's like purchasing a car on the web without test driving it."

The receptionist looked down at the phone and rolled her eyes. "I'm sorry. I was just offering you the different services we provide, for your very own convenience."

"Don't be sorry. Just be careful when you are speaking to a future resident. I'm sure the owner wouldn't appreciate that."

"Absolutely."

"I do have some questions for you, such as security and if anyone could just walk in and make their way around. I need to make sure I'm safe at all times."

"I totally understand that." Alyssa went on to explain how the operation worked, out of fear that her superior would receive a bad report on her. She had already been written up once. Alyssa couldn't afford another. So, she provided the disgruntled customer all the info she requested.

Once all of her questions were answered, she left their residence. It wouldn't be much longer before Gotti sniffed out her lies. As she hopped back on the highway, she dialed another number.

"Hello," Dominic answered.

"Mr. Big Dick King, how are you?"

Dominic was taken back by the inappropriate greeting. "Who is this?"

"The pussy that's going to set you free."

"I'm going to hang up if you don't tell me who this is." Dominic was frustrated with the games.

Kendra laughed loudly into the phone. "It's me, Kendra. How could you not recognize my voice after that amazing night we had together?"

"We didn't have shit. You drugged me."

"Boo-hoo. You sound just like your wife. I just wanted to spice things up a bit and show you what you've been missing."

"Goodbye, Kendra. I don't have time for your games."

"If you hang up this phone, I promise you I will call Storm and tell her we fucked. I'm sure you didn't disclose that information to her as of yet."

Dominic sighed and clutched his weapon that rested in his lap. If it wasn't Gotti playing games, it was crazy ass Kendra and frankly, he was tired of both of them. "What do you want Kendra?" The venom in his voice laced his words.

"I want to see you." Kendra rubbed between her legs. "And finish what we left off."

"We didn't leave off anywhere. That was you and your deceptive ways. I should've known better. Especially after the stunt you pulled."

Kendra stopped at a red light, closed her eyes and bit down on her bottom lip. "I would love to pull on something else."

"Kendra! Just stop," he shouted.

"I can't. I'm addicted to you." She purred.

"I'm not sleeping with you, Kendra."

"You either meet me tonight at my place or I will ruin your pathetic little marriage. And Dominic, that's a promise. Not a threat."

"Yeah."

Kendra blew kisses in the phone. "See you at nine, baby, and don't be late."

After her little fiasco, Kendra made her way to the soul food restaurant and placed an order for her and Gotti. The only thoughts swimming through her mind was sinking her claws into Dominic in the next few hours. The cashier called Kendra's name multiple times before she finally snapped out of her trance.

"Kendra," the cashier called out once more and placed the food beside the register.

150

Finally jumping up from her seat, she approached the counter and snatched her bag before walking out the door. In Kendra's mind, she felt that if she and Gotti were going to run off together, she needed to feel Dominic one last time and she would be satisfied.

Arriving back to Gotti's grandmother's house, Kendra pulled her car around to the backyard and got out. Stepping up to the back door, she paused as Gotti walked out with his pistol aimed.

"Can you please lower that fucking gun? I'm not trying to be a statistic like your little officer friends."

"Maybe I shoulda just shot yo complaining ass. Come in the damn house," Gotti snapped, while stepping to the side so she could enter. "Did you handle that business? What did it look like?" he asked, speaking on Dominic and Storm's new residence.

Kendra's mind had to think quickly because Gotti was highly intelligent. If there was any stumble, he would clearly be able to tell if she was lying. Dominic wasn't ready for the plot she was devising and Storm was gonna receive the shitty end of the stick.

"That place is crawling with cops. They were everywhere. Not to mention, you're on everyone's dashboard for trying to massacre those cops. Don't you think that was stupid? I mean, that's kinda putting a pause on the mission at hand, don't ya think?" she asked before eating a hand full of fries.

"Shut the hell up. You don't have to remind me, Kendra. I've been pondering on a way to do this without alerting anyone. This isn't a damn house. If I walk inside of that building, I may not make it back out, which will be bad for whoever's around. I'm not going back to prison," he mugged with his pistol still in hand.

"Well, that's kinda clear to see, but Dominic is not about to let her go. What makes you think she's going to just hand her child over like that?"

"You mean my child."

Kendra couldn't do anything, but stare as he circled around the living room in deep thought. It was never a game unless more than one participated to play. Unfortunately, she was the player that would rather break the rules before losing.

Standing up, Kendra moved towards him until they stood face-to-face. Wasting no time, she dropped to her knees and dug inside of his pants. Releasing his manhood, Kendra began to give him the sloppiest head possible. It was quite easy to get an angry man at ease. Gotti's mind was so stuck on the catastrophe between him and Storm that he was blinded from the grand picture.

Gripping the back of her head, Gotti pushed down harder. The sounds of her gagging on his member caused him to fuck her mouth as if she was throwing the pussy back. It didn't take long for her to drain the life out of his rod. After five minutes of non-stop tongue action, Kendra felt his knees slightly buckle.

"Why you wanna do this shit right now when you know where my mind at?" Gotti questioned through low eyes.

"Because you're like a mad man when you're not getting your dick sucked. You're moving too fast and I'm trying to get you to listen so we can end this. You won't take my advice."

Taking a seat on the couch, he exhaled deeply. "Kendra, I don't take advice from people, because I always end up losing. No one can dictate how I move, because I move the best. It's been that way my whole life, ma. I ain't just start acting like this."

Crawling next to him, she placed her feet over his legs. "But you've never listened to me either. How do you know if my plan isn't gonna work?"

Looking into her eyes, Gotti smirked. "What, Kendra?"

"Thank you. Now we both know running into that place to get these two is gonna be bad for business. They've probably already warned the front desk about you and got the feds on speed dial. Dominic isn't letting Storm move around, period. Trust me. I know him. Now, if we can lead him away from her and let me handle the front desk. I can slide past and go up to retrieve Rain from this bitch."

"What did I tell you about that bitch word?"

"Do you want me and the baby or do you want Storm?" Kendra questioned.

"You know what the fuck I want."

"So as I said, this bitch will not be able to stop me from handling that. Your only problem will be Dominic because he's gonna try and kill you about this."

"Dominic is a bitch. The only reason he ain't dead now is because you didn't give me the damn address the first time."

"That's past tense. I can get him to leave. He wants your head and that's the ticket to finesse him out of the building. You call and tell him to meet you. His pride will be in the way and he's gonna bite it. You took his money. You fucked his wife. You had a child with her. This would be the last stand between you two. You're gonna tell him to face you like a man and end it. Meet up and handle the problem however he chooses. It makes it a win-win for you. He respects your gangsta, but he's also intimidated, because you're a young reckless individual. Coming at him with humbleness and an offer to talk the problem out will be the way. He's not gonna pass a chance up to end this beef, because he wants to move on with his family."

Smiling, Gotti leaned over and kissed her lips. "That's probably the smartest shit you've said since I've been with you."

"Fuck you," Kendra giggled. "That's supposed to be my job. I told you to listen. You can't beat everybody with aggression. Dominic is a boss. He only wants to deal with people that carry themselves accordingly. The one thing he knows is you're a killer. He wouldn't pass this opportunity to squash this beef and move on. While you're handling that however you choose, I'll be sliding out of that building with your child, heading back to you. We both win."

"That sounds great, but how are we gonna do that if I don't have the number?"

"It's inside of my phone." Kendra grinned evilly.

"Bring yo ass here," he chuckled before climbing on top of her.

Pulling her pants from her body, he stared with lust in his eyes. "After we handle this tomorrow, we're gonna be twenty-four hours away from living stress-free."

"I believe you." She fiddled with his pants.

Kendra's mind was racing on what was next to come. Her plot was falling together smoothly and if all evened out right, then she would be the one with the prize. Feeling Gotti slide inside her warm kitty, she closed her eyes, picturing how Dominic would be fucking her skin off within the next few weeks. Life was great and there was more to come after all her pawns were out of the picture.

Chapter 19

Standing in the parking lot of their home, Clyde stood behind the officers who crowded around in a small circle. After arriving home a few hours ago, he noticed the kicked-in door and instantly alerted the authorities. His heart was unsettled. Tia was pregnant with his child and the recent beef between Dominic and Gotti placed her in jeopardy. She warned him numerous times to pack up and leave, but the heartache he suffered between the two men caused him to push for more. Clyde wanted to be compensated for the drama or he was willing to make it to where everyone besides him lost horribly. The same horrible thought process was now haunting him back, because everyone was clueless on whether his child's mother still had her life at the time.

"Mr. Daniels, when is the last time you saw your wife?"

Rubbing a hand across his head, he pondered. "About six hours ago. I left to go and handle a few things. She was okay."

"And can you tell me your whereabouts at the time, while you weren't here?"

"Excuse me? Are you looking for my wife or is this an interrogation?"

"Sir, I'm only doing my job."

"Well, it damn sure doesn't seem like it. My pregnant woman is out there somewhere and you're trying to attack my character."

"Wells, it's okay, I got it from here," Detective Saunders said before stepping over to Clyde. "I'm gonna need you to calm down just for a second, so we can fix this and get your wife back to you."

"This is bigger than you understand, Saunders," he replied, taking a seat on the porch.

"Explain."

"I just need to make sure my wife is straight. There's a reason you guys have me under this witness protection program. To protect. No one is doing their fucking job and Tia could be dead for all we know."

"First of all, calm the fuck down. Whatever is going on with your wife, you need to check yourself, because I'm sure you play a major position in all this mess. You're an ex-drug dealer who's mixed in the motion of a lunatic family member who wants you dead. That sums it up for the most part. Correct?"

Watching the nervousness in his posture, Saunders continued. "You're pushing yourself down into a pit that's about to blaze up in the matter of a few seconds. Your criminal record is amazing. It's enough to make sure you can get at least half of the time we have waiting for your cousin. We know about things you try and hide, Mr. Daniels. You and Mr. King's little friend, Juve, the one who was murdered in his home by the hands of his associates. Or what about the drug ring?"

Lowering his head, Clyde began to slightly sweat. "It wasn't my fault. I never wanted to live this life for good. I made my money and got out, man. That's the truth. I just wanted to have my family. Gotti has something to do with this and I'm positive about it. He's trying to kill me and everyone is blind to the fact that he's the problem. Not me."

"I'm afraid that when you're a criminal, Mr. Daniels, there's no such thing as putting the blame on another criminal, unless you're in front of a judge. Since the witness protection program is what you want, we're gonna give it you. Stand up," Saunders ordered, pulling out a set of handcuffs.

"What?"

"Stand to your feet." Rising up, Clyde placed his hands behind his back. "You're under arrest for the murder of Jeff Harrison. Anything you say can be used for evidence in the court of law. If you don't have an attorney, one will be appointed to you."

"Wait, I didn't kill Juve! My cousin did."

"And you can tell that to the judge at your first court appearance." Placing him inside the back of a police cruiser, Saunders stopped an officer in his tracks and ordered them to transfer him to the Cobb County Jail.

"Detective Saunders. You have a phone call," his assistant shouted.

Grabbing the cell phone, he placed it to his ear. "This is Saunders."

"Are you observing the same thing I am?" Juan asked curiously.

"What do you mean? You made it seem to me as if these little people could help us accomplish a case and it led us nowhere. The captain wants us back to the unit right now. I suggest you find a way to make it there," Saunders stated before ending the call.

* * *

Sitting up, Kendra rolled out of the bed. Glancing over at Gotti who slept peacefully on his side, she grabbed her cell and headed out of the room. It was two thirty in the morning and the cold breeze lingering outside caressed her bare thighs, as she stepped out on the back porch. Dialing Dominic's number, she waited patiently for an answer.

"Why are you calling my phone, Kendra? I've already told you there's nothing to talk about," he whispered through the line.

"That's where you're wrong, because there's a lot to talk about sir. We have unfinished business and I'm the only one who can help solve that for you."

"You're a fucking pest. My woman has been through enough, dealing with you and all the other fake, wannabe-ass friends of hers. Why can't you guys just get a life?"

"Dominic, that was the sweetest thing anyone has ever said to me. I know this may be hard to understand, so I'll try my best to make it this clear."

"No! I'll make this clear for you, bitch. I'm done playing these childish games with you and everyone else. My woman doesn't want to be friends with you. She doesn't want to forgive you. Our life is great and I'm working very hard on not peeling you and Gotti's brains back. I've gave warning after warning and you're still pushing that button," he spat closing the door to their bedroom, so he wouldn't wake Storm.

Kendra smiled. "Are you done? Because if you are, I can tell you the important shit that needs to be said, unless you don't wanna hear what Gotti is trying to do?"

Hearing his name always left bad thoughts in the air. Gotti was a nigga that meant no good. So, if something was stirring up, Kendra would be the easiest person to deliver his threats. Dominic was well on-point with the game that was being played and being a victim of their treachery was not on the list of things to do.

"I'm listening."

"You're in so deep, Dominic. Gotti wants to make a deal with you, but we all know how the cookie crumbles."

"Mm-hmm. I don't make deals with enemies. What the hell is wrong with you?"

"Nothing is wrong with me. But there is something wrong with him. See, you played with a man that had nothing else to lose. He's delusional about your wife and he has a reason to be. She fucked him numerous times and led him to believe the love they shared was rekindled. She did it in front of me. In front of Tia. She had no shame. It's impossible to blame a man who's been tricked by the hands of a woman with great pussy power. Now you're stuck in the middle, because you're twisted off the same nookie," Kendra snickered.

"Fuck you, bitch. I'm starting to lose my patience with you."

"And I'm starting to feel Storm needs to know you were deep in my fucking guts with all that dick you toting down there. What about that, big daddy? Huh?"

Sighing heavily, Dominic grew quiet. "What the fuck do you want from me?"

"I want you to fix this issue. Gotti would like to have his child back. He doesn't care about your little princess Storm anymore. He also has the four hundred thousand dollars for you. Now as crazy as this may sound, he's gonna try to kill you because he feels you ruined everything he had. He's on the run from every justice department you can think of and he's bound to be dead any day now. Why not by the hands of you?" Kendra asked in a serious tone.

"Why would I have to kill him if the police are willing? That sounds dumb. You really expect me to believe he has my money, when he worked so hard to keep it?

You can run that lie on a slow man, but it won't work on me."

"I have no reason to lie. The same way I just told you he wants to kill you. It's the truth. You have to face the fact this is nobody's fault but Storm's. She started this and now she leaving you to finish it."

"It wasn't her fault. She made a mistake and I'm past that part of our marriage. I just want to move on."

"And I'm telling you how. Kill him and you can have your life again. It's easy."

"And what's in this for you?" Dominic questioned while pacing around the hallway.

"The money, Dominic. I want half. The other two hundred grand is yours. I counted it myself, so I'm positive about the number. After you get rid of him, you get the cash and move on with your life, I keep our little secret and everyone's happy."

"And how can I guarantee that you won't still tell Storm after all this is over?"

"Because you have my word. But, there is one little thing I need you to slide in for me."

"What?"

"I wanna make love to you, Dominic."

"Not gonna happen. I love Storm and I can't hurt her like that. You're pushing it."

"How? I've already had my sample and I know you felt how warm and good my pussy was," she mumbled seductively with her fingers caressing her womanhood.

"If the money is what you want so badly, why do you keep switching it back to what happened between me and you? I never agreed to have sex. You drugged me and took it, Kendra."

"But we're past that now. Just one last time and we can go our separate ways. If this is what can save you and Storm, why not?"

Dominic knew Kendra was insane. Her proposition was stupid, but the pain his family was being put through was placing a hex on their lives. His love for Rain grew by the day, but the truth was something he couldn't run away from. She was still Gotti's child. He knew for a fact that Storm wasn't letting the child leave her sight, especially putting her in the hands of the man who caused so much pain and havoc. The damage was already done and there was no other way to revert it back to what it was.

"So when can we handle this and get it over with?" His mind was racing, but the plan in his head was his last hope.

"Tomorrow. I'll have him to call you, so you both can meet. I would suggest you avoid text messages and be very discreet. He's confused, Dominic, and killing you is the only way he thinks that he can have his child. I can't tell you how to make it work, but if you bring the child, he's gonna be more relaxed. It's the only way."

"I'll be waiting," he agreed before hanging up. Stepping back into the bedroom, Storm stood directly by the door. "Who were you talking to?"

Catching him off guard, Dominic gathered his lie quickly. "It was Jacob's family. I just spoke with his wife. She's taking this issue pretty rough right now," he replied, kissing her forehead.

"Is she okay?"

"No. I don't think so. She lost her life when Jacob passed. He was the glue to their entire family. It's hard to even hold a conversation with her, because I feel I'm the reason she's unhappy."

"That's not true, Dominic. Jacob was your friend and you would never do anything to see him hurt. You're probably the only person who truly cared for him at that dealership."

Looking Storm in the eyes, he grabbed her hand and placed a soft kiss on it. "Can I ask you something?"

"Of course. Is everything okay?" she asked, taking a seat next to him on the king size bed.

Being sure to place his words together correctly, Dominic glanced over to Rain, who slept peacefully in her bassinette. "If Gotti wanted to have his child, would you let him?"

"What? Dominic, what are you talking about? Gotti isn't allowed to be in my child's life. He's reckless and having my baby is definitely out of the question. Dominic, why would you ask me a question like that?"

"Baby, calm down. You're gonna wake Rain." He could tell the question sent her a little over the edge from the way her chest was heaving. "I'm only asking. Have you ever thought she might be the reason he's acting out?"

"He's not, Dominic. He's crazy about me. Rain doesn't matter to him. We tried this. Remember?"

"So, how do you think Rain would feel once she gets older and never meets her biological father?"

"I feel life works that way sometimes, baby. We are all we need and to be honest, she never has to know, because you are perfect enough to lead this family forever. You are all we need." She placed a hand on his cheek.

Smooching her lips, Dominic climbed back into the bed with Storm directly next to him. Rubbing her back, he stared at the ceiling in deep thought. Pulling his gun was a trait that was in his past, but Gotti was about to change that.

* * *

"Tonight, I called you men here for one reason and one reason only. Mr. Daniels is starting to become a problem for this department. His actions have cost over four lives and it has even landed one of your own inside the hospital in critical condition. He's a menace. You men were gathered because I know you are some of the toughest men on this force. We have forty-eight hours to find this man and bring him down, dead or alive. The FBI is trying to come down and swoop in to take this case, which is going to lead all of us to the unemployment line. We have a mission, team. That's to find this guy and bring him to justice for all the grieving families."

"So he's dangerous. Who's not?" one of the officers stated arrogantly.

The small group of officers began to laugh from the remark.

Straightening his glasses, Captain Rodgers silenced them. "I wouldn't give a damn how much experience you guys have had. No one is invincible in this force. Yes. You men are very fit for this mission, but that doesn't mean we can slip on this criminal.

Grabbing the manila folder that sat on his desk, he opened it up. "These are some of the priors the suspect has had within the past eight years. Besides the six aggravated assaults with a deadly weapon, he was tried on an attempted murder and wagged through the system. The next is four armed robberies that led to five people being shot with a semi-automatic weapon. So, with that being said, you will have to be cautious when approaching this man. He's past dangerous. He's taken lives, men, and let's be clear when I say that it could have easily been one of you. Our only job is to make sure we deliver the criminal to the justice system and let them handle their jobs from there. We're focused. We are a team. Not murderers. I've assigned Saunders as the squad captain to ensure that you gentlemen understand the history and format of what's about to take place here tomorrow."

Nodding to him, Captain Rodgers took a seat behind his oak wood desk. Standing to his feet, Saunders stepped in front of the men with a stern expression written across his face.

"Now I know you guys have been working for the past week non-stop, but this is the big fish here. We have a man that's on our radar for doing the most destructive things you could ever imagine. Captain Rodgers is right. He's not a normal man when it comes to crime, but we aren't an ordinary force. So place his words to the back of your head for a second and understand that he's old."

"Don't push it, Saunders." The captain's face was starting to flush bright red.

"No disrespect, sir, but we can't soften the hearts of these men. I have worked for this force for over twenty years and I understand what it takes to bring assholes like this down. We can't play around as if this is a soft matter. This criminal is a madman. He has tried his best to kill officers. The same men you work with. I don't know about you men, but that makes me angry. I say we have twenty-four hours to find this man and put an end to this before it's too late. Within forty-eight hours, we will be losing our careers for this bomb and I'm not about to sit around and let that happen. We meet back here in the a.m.

and we're heading out to catch this guy. If he makes us kill him, justice will be served. I advise you men to get some rest because we have a serious day ahead of us tomorrow," Saunders said before dismissing the force.

As everyone started to depart, Juan stood to his feet and approached the front. I'm guessing you forgot to tell them that Daniels has kidnapped this woman?"

"No. I didn't forget. Right now it wasn't necessary. We have the authority to proceed with taking this guy down and the rest will unfold as we go."

"You know it's against protocol to put a citizen's life in danger. What are you trying to do here, Saunders?"

"I'm trying to catch a fucking bad guy. This man has caused enough pain and drama and if that means we lose one to save hundreds, then I'm willing to proceed."

"Hey! What the hell is wrong with you two?" Captain Rodgers asked, stepping in between them.

"I refuse to be a part of something like this. He's not being considerate of the lives that are at stake here. You walk around flaunting your little medals as if you earned them like a true detective. You're planning to assassinate this man for your own benefit!"

"What the hell do you care if he lives or dies, Juan? Huh? Are you working with him or us? Because this department hasn't had your help in a very long time with ceasing the violence. I have a job to do. If he gives up, he will make it to live another day. If not, that will be another problem handled for this squad. We leave out in the morning. With or without you," Saunders yelled before dismissing himself.

Shaking his head, Juan switched his attention over to Captain Rodgers. "You're letting him proceed with the intentions to murder this man? You are the lead of this department and you're promoting corruption sir."

"Juan, what other choice do we have? We've had patience with this guy and now it's coming down to the boiling point of no return. In the next few days, you won't have a job to love anymore if we don't get this guy off of the streets. I've worked hard for this position and I didn't make it here to lose it by a young punk who wants to rampage and renegade. He has to be stopped."

Pondering to himself, Juan thought about Gotti's issues and knew his story was one that couldn't be understood by his co-workers. He knew things Captain Rodgers couldn't see and in order to save the life of the innocent people involved, Juan would have to take matters into his own hands.

"You're going to make the wrong decision and it's going to backfire on you harder than a busted motor. Innocent people are about to perish from the hands of the same men who are supposed to protect and serve. I will not be one of those men, sir," Juan stated before removing his badge. Placing it on Captain Rodgers' desk, Juan turned to the door and walked out.

Chapter 20

Walking inside the room where Tia sat bound to a chair, Gotti cracked the blinds, letting the bright sun caress her face. Jumping from her sleep, she stared at him with a hateful expression.

"Gotti?"

Looking down at her, he stopped in his tracks. "What?"

"Why are you doing this? I've never wished any bad on you, Gotti. I wanted you to get your life back with Storm. She wanted to move on," Tia whispered with a raspy voice.

Pulling a cold bottle of Dasani water from his back pocket, he popped the seal and placed it to her lips. As she drank, he continued to watch her with curious eyes. After quenching her thirst, Gotti placed the water on the floor and took a seat in the chair directly across from her.

"You know, when I was younger, I used to bring Storm over here to be around my family. It was like she adapted to my people easily, which made me know she was meant just for me. I cherished everything about her. The beauty. Her mind. Even the love she gave when I consisted to be an asshole," he chuckled. "It was like she never left, because my love was genuine. It was real, ya know. Now it's like my whole entire world crashed down in a matter of months. The same woman I cherished and gave my all to is married. She's with a man I've killed for. I feel like the biggest lame ever."

"Storm never meant took hurt you, Gotti. She was mad about Jade. It pushed her to do what she did and you can't blame her. Storm loved you so much that she practically gave up on our friendship. She felt betrayed about

Jade and placed that hurt on me and Kendra. We suffered because of something she did. I know the story, Gotti. I know it wasn't your fault."

Sitting back with a sad expression, Gotti leaned forward. "Can I tell you something, Tia?"

"Yes. You can tell me anything. I've been friends with you for years Gotti. Regardless of your fallouts with Storm."

"I wanted you all to be the bridesmaids at our wedding. The time I sat in prison, I knew I was coming home to ask Storm for her hand in marriage. She meant the world to me, so when I came home to a wedding ring on her finger, it crushed me. I waited to see if it was just a phase, to see if she may come back to me one day. It made me lash out in ways I didn't want to. She was my heart."

Gotti laughed with light tears in his eyes. "But I guess I'm the one who suffered behind that, you know. It never fails. Regardless of how much of a good man I could've been, I would have never been able to explain what occurred between me and Jade, in order to get Storm to believe me. So this is the way I have to be, Tia. I know it's not fair, but what other choice do I have? Storm and my daughter is the only thing that helps me breathe and it's gone. Where does that leave me?" he asked before standing back to his feet.

"There's still hope, Gotti. Just because you have lost doesn't mean that you can't change things. You're a great person in my eyes regardless of how many mistakes you have made. But doing irrational things will not make it better."

"I'm afraid it is what it is. Dominic has crossed the line and he's trailing on a thin road that's about to crumble. He can have Storm, because shit will never be the same. I just want you to tell her that I loved her and no matter what, I'm gonna take care of the child. She's gonna be raised the right way. I promise."

"What are you about to do, Gotti? Please don't hurt anyone else."

"After this is over, I'll make sure you get home safe," he mentioned before leaving out of the room. Heading into the living area, Kendra sat on the couch with a confident smile.

"Are you ready to put this behind us?"

"Yeah. After I take care of this nigga, make sure you stop back here and let Tia loose. I don't wanna see nothing happen to her."

"If that's what you want." Kendra shrugged her shoulders.

"What time is it?"

"It's one-twenty-four. Time is moving fast," she replied.

"What time does this nigga wanna meet? I don't wanna spook him and give him any clue of what's about to happen."

"He said nine. There's an abandoned Church's Chicken on Bankhead. It's the perfect spot and it's secluded. It'll be easy. You can grab Rain and leave his ass back there. I felt that it was the perfect area. The police ain't answering no calls about gunshots in that area anyway."

"Perfect. I need you to meet me at the airport at midnight. Don't be late, because our flight leaves at one am."

"You know I got you, daddy," she agreed before placing a kiss on his lips.

Leaving out of the back door, Gotti and Kendra locked down the house and jumped into their separate cars. Pulling out of the driveway, Detective Juan sat across the street with his camera catching the two as they turned out into the street. Cranking his car, he slowly pulled away making sure to keep a distance. Alerting the department would probably cause chaos, so that was out of the question. It was only one way to bring Gotti in and that was to have patience and take the opportunity when the time presented itself.

* * *

Waking up from her sleep, Storm climbed out of her bed. Heading into the front room of their presidential suite, she found Dominic sitting on the couch in deep thought. He sported an all- black sweat suit with a pair of black Nikes. It looked as if he was back in his twenties, instead of pushing forty years old.

"Baby, are you okay?" She asked, taking a seat next to him.

Breaking his trance, Dominic kissed her lips. "Yeah, I'm okay."

Storm could tell from his dry response that something was wrong. He was never the type to sit around and be depressed about anything, so his actions gave away that there was surely a problem.

"Dominic, lately you have been really down. Are you sure there's nothing going on?" Storm was now grabbing his face so he could look into her eyes.

"Yes. I'm going to take Rain out for a ride and get a little air. I have a little business to attend to, so I'm gonna let you get some rest while me and the baby spend some time together," he said before grabbing her baby bag. Rain was already dressed and prepared to go.

"Can I ride?"

"Not today, love. This is a daddy and daughter moment." Dominic said with a fake smile. Truth be told, he didn't want Storm to be involved with what was about to take place. It was the only way to ensure that she would be safe and unaware of his mission.

"Okay, fine. I need me some mommy time anyway. I'll sit back and watch me a couple of movies with a big bowl of ice cream by myself," she laughed before kissing his cheek.

"I love you," Dominic said, as he picked up Rain's car seat to leave.

"I love you too, baby."

Stepping in the hallway, Dominic headed to the elevator and pulled out his cellphone. Dialing a number, he placed it up to his ear. "Dominic. What's good, my brother?"

"I'm on the way to the plaza. I'll be there in twenty minutes.
I'll be waiting."

Hearing the answer he needed, he hung up and prepared himself for what was about to occur. It was nearly thirty minutes later when Dominic pulled his truck inside of the Walmart parking lot. Sliding next to his friend's Tahoe, he grabbed the baby and climbed out.

"Matt. It's good to see you again, bro. I wanna let you know that I really appreciate this."

"Come on, Dominic. You know I ain't gotta problem doing you a favor after everything you sacrificed for me. Hell, my kids will love to be around the little baby right now. They need something to keep they bad ass occupied."

Smiling, Dominic handed Rain over to him. "I'll call you as soon as I'm finished."

"Sure thing, bro." Watching Matt place Rain into his Tahoe, Dominic waited until his friend pulled out of the huge parking lot before going into the store. Heading inside the Walmart, he moved around until he found the toy section.

***

Detective Juan checked the time on his watch as he followed Gotti around the streets of Atlanta. It was hard to know he was moving around with the dark tinted windows that covered his identity. After Kendra split apart and drove her separate way, he decided to follow Gotti. It was too much of a risk to let him out of sight with all that was sitting on the table. The whereabouts of Clyde Daniels' wife was still a puzzle and he could possibly lead him directly to her if he waited patiently to see his next move.

Sliding inside of Clyde's parking lot of his home, Gotti tossed on his hoodie before climbing out of his whip. Being sure that his pistol was off safety and tucked, he continued to the backyard of the home.

"Damn it!" Detective Juan cursed after spotting him disappear into the back of his cousin's home. Gotti was now out of sight and there would be no positive answer on what he was doing until he reappeared.

Sliding into the back of Clyde's open shed, Gotti stepped in and pulled a large suitcase from the bottom of his tool shelf. Opening it up, he grabbed a hand full of blue Benjamin's and pulled the rubber band from around it. Thumbing through it, he placed over ten grand in his pocket and closed the case. Leaving out of the shed, Gotti made his way back to the car and tossed the money inside of the trunk with his other duffle.

The hustling game did him major justice for the short time he'd been out of prison. No one, not even Clyde knew he had over a half-a-million dollars stashed behind his home. It was the cash he was saving to build his family back with Storm. After shit went sour, he knew his actions would lead to him ducking it off for a while. *Now it's time to end my journey and create a new one,* Gotti thought, before pulling back out on the road with Detective Juan directly behind him. It was one last stop he needed to make before he ended his mission.

* * *

5:30 pm

Pulling into the cemetery, Gotti stepped out of his car and made his way up to his grandmother's tombstone. Staring at her name on the slab of concrete, he kneeled down. "Hey, Big Mama. I know it's been a while, huh?"

Rubbing his fingers across the grass, he smiled. "I hate when I come to see you like this. I haven't been myself lately, Mama. Storm left me. She's actually married to another man and feels that your great granddaughter shouldn't see me. It hurts so bad, but guess what, Mama? I'm ending it all tonight. I know you're disappointed in the way I've been carrying myself, but I lost track. I was blinded and wasn't focused. I've decided to let Storm be, because I know that you really had love for her. You wouldn't want me to cause harm to her, but her little boyfriend can't be so lucky, Mama."

Staring at the sky, Gotti wiped his tears. "I refuse to be played like a bitch. I gave my heart to this girl. I know you would cherish my child, as if she was your own. She looks just like me. We have a new part of our bloodline. I hate it's ending this way, but I promise I will keep her safe. I'm not gonna be able to come and see you for a while and I don't want you to think I would ever forget about you. These people are looking for me, Mama and if I don't leave, they're gonna try and kill me. I'm not about to let them take me away from you. If this dude doesn't come off my daughter, I'm gonna have to handle my business. It's either him or me," Gotti said before standing to his feet. "I love you mama." Kissing her headstone, he made his way back to the car. Feeling his phone vibrate, Gotti pulled it out of his pocket and answered. "What is it?"

"You need to be prepared. Dominic texted my phone and said that he's getting ready, so make sure you're on time. Handle him and get it over with."

"Good. I'm about to smoke me a blunt and get ready now. Be sure you remember what I said, twelve o'clock."

"I heard you, Gotti. Be careful," Kendra spoke before hanging up.

Getting in his car, he sparked a joint and turned his music on. Tonight was it. The rush that was pumping through his veins gave him that energy he needed. It was no turning back. Pondering on the way Storm crossed him out, he began to grow angry. Inhaling the weed heavily, he started his engine. The hatred for his enemy was pumping hard and now it was time to can those feelings forever. It was either him or Gotti and it surely wasn't an obituary for Greg Daniels anywhere in sight.

* * *

9:10 pm.

As darkness swallowed the bright blue sky, Dominic stood with his car parked behind the abandoned Church's Chicken. The wind was pushing heavy and it was ten minutes past the time limit. His adrenaline was pumping and he was beginning to lose patience. Just as he whipped out his cellphone to call Kendra, a set of headlights slowly pulled inside the entrance of the restaurant. Making sure he had easy access to his pistol, Dominic crossed his arms just as Gotti's car came to a halt. Watching him step out, they stood twenty feet away from each other.

"Where the fuck is my baby?"

"Where the fuck is my money, nigga?" Dominic shot back with more aggression.

Smirking, Gotti opened his trunk and pulled out the black Gucci duffle. Tossing it towards him, it landed a few feet away from his shoes. Being sure to move cautiously, Dominic opened the back car door and pulled Rain's car seat from the vehicle. Holding the seat with gentleness, he eyed Gotti.

"How can I ensure my wife will see her baby again?"

"That's a question I don't have time to try and explain. Hand over my kid, nigga. A deal is a deal."

Taking a deep breath, Dominic started to move forward.

* * *

Strolling through the lobby of The Huntley residence, Kendra eased her way onto the elevator. After reaching the top floor, she exited out of the doors and made a sharp left. It wasn't hard to find the top presidential suite in the entire building, especially after a worker was willing to ease out a little info for a hundred-dollar-bill.

All of that was paid for with the cool thirty grand she greased from Gotti's duffle the morning before. Reaching her destination, Kendra clutched her chrome pistol and knocked sternly on the door. It wasn't even a matter of seconds before she heard Storm fumbling in the room.

"I'm coming. I'm coming. Dominic, if you left your key, I'm gonna kick your ass." As she opened the door, the handle of Kendra's gun sent her crashing to the floor.

"Mrs. King, did you happen to order some room service?" she grinned wickedly before stepping in and closing the door behind her. Holding her face, Storm stared up into her ex best friend's eyes.

"Kendra. What the fuck are you doing here? What is your problem?" Storm said, breathing harshly. The gash in the side of her head was pouring blood and all she could do was crawl backwards.

"My problem?" Kendra giggled. "I don't know, Storm, let's see. I'll try and refresh your memory a little."

Strolling through the plaza, Storm and Kendra headed to get their daily meal, while on their lunch break from the hospital. "Girl, so wassup for tonight? Are we calling Jade and Tia to smash out to this new bar or what?"

"Bitch, you know I'm not too good with the whole club thing. People have a tendency to shoot and do dumb shit while we're trying to have fun. It kills the whole mood," Storm replied, sipping on her smoothie.

"Girl, ain't nobody worried about dying. If anything, I'ma pop this ass on a nigga and make him kill his damn self," Kendra laughed, while twerking in her tight scrubs.

Giggling at her friend, Storm shook her head. "You a mess." Their conversation was interrupted as Dominic walked in front of them with his hands inside his beige slacks.

"Girl, that's who I was telling you about. That's my chocolate crush," Kendra said, with nervousness taking over her.

"Ooooh, I think I do remember seeing him a few times. I think he's waiting for you," Storm whispered.

"Excuse me. How are you ladies doing? I don't mean to just walk up without y'all permission, but do you mind if I have a word with you for a minute, beautiful?" he asked, looking down in Storm's eyes.

Looking over at Kendra with a wide mouth, Storm stepped backwards. "Don't you mean you wanna speak to my friend?"

"Uhh. No disrespect, but I know exactly who I was talking too. I mean you." He pointed at Storm directly.

Watching Kendra's expression change, she took a step back. "I'm sorry, but my friend likes you. I'm gonna have to pass, but it would be a pleasure if you could just give her a chance," Storm smiled, showing her pearly whites.

"Mm-hmm. Maybe I can just catch you at a different time." He winked his eye without replying to her last comment.

Watching him walk off, Kendra folded her arms. "This is great. He sees you one time and now he's in love. Damn, bitch, why is everybody so attracted to you? This nigga know I'm horny in the pants for his ass."

"Girl, don't make me laugh. I'm not about to talk to his ass, so he gonna have to come in sooner or later. You're my friend, bitch. I'm not about to step on your toes with Mr. Rico Suave," Storm snickered.

"Thanks, baby girl. Hell, I may need to put that Kendra special on his ass. He'll be craving hard then," she joked as they walked off to grab their lunch.

* * *

Sitting the car seat down, Dominic stepped back as Gotti moved forward. Pulling the cover off of her car seat, Gotti's eyes grew wide in anger after spotting the baby doll that rested in his baby's place. His head rose just as Dominic pulled the gun from his hip. The bullet he released struck Gotti in the arm, sending him to the concrete.

Boc!

His reflexes moved in a flash. Before Dominic could pull the trigger again, Gotti's pistol was out, letting off shots recklessly.

Boc! Boc! Boc! Boc! Boc!

One of the slugs quickly found a home in Dominic's shoulder, causing him to dodge behind the large metal dumpster.

"Fuck nigga, you dead!" Gotti yelled jumping to his feet. His gun continued to pop, as he waited for Dominic to show his face. Sitting behind the trash can, he took deep breaths and listened as his shots ricocheted off the container. Trying to peep his head out, a bullet nearly grazed his head. The blood from his shoulder was pouring profusely, sending pain through the left side of his body. Easing his mind, Dominic continued to count the shots while gripping his gun. After the next two shots from Gotti's gun, rang out, he stepped from behind the dumpster and placed a shot directly to the center of his chest.

Boom!

Watching him crash to the ground, Dominic slowly walked over and kicked his pistol across the concrete. Gotti was breathing erratically and his chest sported a hole big enough to drop a quarter through. Looking in his eyes, Dominic shook his head. "I warned you, nigga. I told you to stay away."

"Fuck you, nigga! I can never die," Gotti mumbled, as the blood started to pour from his mouth.

Taking a deep breath, Dominic gripped his shoulder. "I told you, lil nigga, when we first met. It's a difference between a street nigga and a killer. Releasing four more shots into his face, Dominic stared down at his lifeless body. The pain Gotti caused was horrible. It was drama that Dominic never expected to cross his path and now it was finally over. Climbing back in the car, he tossed a thin jacket over his Nike hoodie and pulled out of the lot. Letting him cross the stoplight, Detective Juan crunk his car up and began to follow him.

* * *

"So now you know, Storm. You know why your best friend is here to blow your brains out, inside of the bathtub. Get yo ass up," she spat with her eyes slanted. "You crossed me out and now I'm here to take your life. You're

Destiny Skai & Chris Green

living my dream. You married my man. You spending my money and I'm gonna take it all back. Get the fuck up!" she screamed.

Storm stood to her feet as Kendra held the gun pointed towards her face. "Maybe I should just kill you right here, huh?" Storm remained quiet in fear of being shot.

"Mm-hmm. I think I will. I wish you good luck in hell, bitch," Kendra whispered before trying to pull the trigger. Noticing the gun wouldn't fire, she began to panic. Spotting her chance, Storm rushed her for the weapon. As the two women struggled to gain the gun, Storm delivered a hard punch to Kendra's gut. Watching the pistol fall to the floor, Storm pushed her towards the patio window.

Stumbling through the glass, Kendra's body tumbled over the small guard rail, sending her down a hundred-foot fall. Turning her head, Storm's eyes began to pour tears before rushing towards the phone.

* * *

Tuning into The Huntley, Dominic stopped his car after spotting the red and blue lights that surrounded the parking lot. Pulling down to the building, he climbed out of his vehicle. Storm instantly flashed through his mind. Rushing through the crowd, he began to push people out of his way.

"Excuse me. Please let me through." He moved carefully, trying not to bump his shoulder. After making it to the front, his eyes caught sight of Storm, sitting on the back of an ambulance bumper. Moving under the caution tape, three officers tried to stop him.

"Hey, sir. You can't cross here."

"That's my wife. That's my wife. Get the fuck off me." He buffed up with anger. Stepping out of the way, they watched as he ran to Storm's side.

"Oh my god, baby, what happened?" He caressed her face.

Pointing over to Kendra's dead body, he quickly turned his head from the sight of her laying on the ground.

"I'm so sorry. I didn't mean to leave you here, Storm. It's my fault, baby." He hugged her with pain rushing through his body.

Looking in her eyes, he whispered, "We have to leave. Now."

Nodding, she climbed off the back of the ambulance just as Detective Saunders walked up to them. "Sir, may I ask who you are?"

"I'm Dominic King and this is my wife."

"I'm guessing you have no clue on what's going on here?"

"Sir, to be honest, I don't want to find out. I would like to get my wife to the hospital, so we can put this behind us."

"Continue," he said with a curious expression before heading back through the crime scene. As Dominic walked through the lot with Storm by his side, Detective Juan rose from the hood of his car. Locking eyes with him, Dominic froze in place.

"Mr. King. It looks like you're hurt." He motioned towards his shoulder. The small spots of blood were slowly seeping tough the fabric. "Where were you just coming from when you pulled inside the residence?" he asked calmly.

Not sure what to say, Dominic lowered his vision. "Detective. I've had a really hard day and my wife is going through a tragic moment right now. I just want to get her to the hospital. Please," he said with sincerity in his tone.

Standing with a moment of silence, Juan stepped to the side. Moving past, he took a deep breath as they made it to the car.

"Dominic, where is Rain?" Storm asked, wanting to hold her child. The incident was a near-death experience and all she wanted to do was be around her two loved ones.

"We're going to pick her up after we leave the hospital. She's safe."

"Baby. You're bleeding. What happened?" she asked, looking at his face.

Cranking the car, Dominic ignored her question and pulled away from the residence's parking lot.

* * *

Standing in the day room of the Cobb County Jail, Clyde watched the TV in shock, as the news reporter spoke with Detectives Juan and Saunders.

"We aren't quite sure about the incident that took place at The Huntley tonight, but we are positive it had a connection with the suspect, Clyde Daniels. Apparently after getting a phone call from across town, we discovered Mr. Daniels shot dead behind the back of a Church's Chicken parking lot."

Gripping his head, Clyde lowered his vision after hearing Gotti's name. Hearing that he was gone placed one person in his mind. *Dominic.*

"Is there anything else you would like to share, Detective Juan?" The reporter asked.

"Yes. After finding Mr. Daniels we retraced his steps and found the missing woman inside of his grandmother's empty home. She was unharmed and taken to the hospital to be treated for any problems with her unborn child. I'm sorry for the lives that this has caused, but now I feel we can push this issue behind us all, now that he is gone for good. That'll be all," Juan replied, before walking off.

"Yes," Clyde mumbled to himself about the news of Tia. It felt great to know his girl was going to be good. It was a sad case about Gotti, but his life was on borrowed time with the actions he was taking. Walking to his room, he laid down on the rough metal bunk. There was nothing more that he could do, besides let the time pass and wish for the best on making it back to his family.

Chapter 21

Montego Bay
Six months later

Sliding back inside the parking lot of their amazing resort, Storm shut off her engine. The sound of her phone vibrating paused her actions of getting out. Spotting the private number, she answered the call. "Who is this?"

"Hey Storm. It's me."

Leaning back in seat, she smiled. "Tia?"

"Yes. It's me, Storm. How are you?"

"I can't complain. I'm living. I still have my life and my daughter. That's enough to be happy about."

"True. I'm so happy you're doing well. I'm not gonna lie, I miss you. I'm in Atlanta by myself and it's kind of pushing me to just leave also ya know. My baby girl is one month now and I need to focus on what can make her happy and straight."

"I'm glad for you too, Tia. Now you know how it feels to be a mother. 'Cause it damn sure ain't easy."

"Girl, you ain't never lied about that. I have enough on my hands with my one, so you know ain't nothing else going on. The single mommy life is true."

"What's going on with Clyde? Is he taking care of his fatherly duties?"

"Storm, Clyde has life in prison. He's never coming home. So I'm guessing I gotta put on them big girl panties and take up that slack."

Shaking her head, Storm said a silent prayer for her. "I hope things work out for you, Tia."

"I saw what happened to Gotti."

Hearing his name sent chills down her spine. It was a couple days after the incident with her and Kendra, when she finally turned on the television. She sat and watched the article on the news about Gotti being assassinated behind a fast food restaurant. It was hard to think about him being dead, but the truth was undeniable. He needed to be deleted from society. Gotti was running loose and a tragedy was bound to overtake everyone, if he would have stuck around a second longer.

After studying Dominic's movements for the past few months, Storm truly began to wonder about his secrets. She even had the guts to ask Dominic if he murdered Gotti. The only thing he would give her was a kiss on the cheek and a smile. The action spooked her, but it also was a turn on for her soft, sweet spot. It was for sure that Dominic would protect her by any means, even if it meant handling an issue himself.

"I'm sorry about Gotti, but Tia, that's my past."

"He spoke to me that night before he died. He actually cried and told me something I never thought would spill from a person like him."

Wondering what she meant, Storm couldn't help but to ask. "What are you talking about? What did he tell you?"

"He told me about you."

"And?"

"The reason he was acting crazy was because he came home to you married. He wanted to come home and ask you to marry him, Storm. He poured out his feelings. That he wanted to have a child with you and build his family. But he was too late. After giving you Rain, he felt that there was a chance. That there was hope you two could be together again. He said you wanted to leave with his

188

child and let her be raised by another man. It drove him insane."

"That's very touching and I'm sorry Gotti couldn't fix that problem. He held in anger because of my actions and I'm sorry I led him on with things I shouldn't have done. I'm on my religious life hard now and Allah tells you that certain things are decreed to happen. When life grows, another one goes, especially when you have your share of the forbidden world. He was lost, Tia, and no matter how much I loved him, he would've wanted more."

"I understand, Storm, and I feel your pain. I hated all this bullshit even happened. Kendra surprised me and it shows me now that we really can't trust everyone who say they love you."

"This is just some real shit, Tia. Fuck Kendra. She did that to herself and it's the way life works, as I just said. We all have a destiny to see and I refuse to be a bum in the world with a bunch of ignorant people. I invested into this resort that I'm living in and me and Dominic are nearly partial owners. We invested our fortune into the place where my child will grow to be the best. It's better to leave and strive for yourself."

"I really appreciate that, Storm. My heart is at ease and I know I have my mind together. You know I don't want you to be a stranger. I'm still your friend."

"I'll always love you. But right now, I'm focused on being a mother, a business woman and a wife. If the right time presents itself, I'll be sure to pull through and check on you."

"Thanks. I'll keep in touch, Storm. I promise."

"Alahamdulilah."

Ending the call, Storm stepped out of the car and inhaled deeply. Smoothing out her Dolce and Gabbana slacks, she slid into her Gucci sandals and closed the door. It was like a breath of fresh air. To be free. To be alive again. Dominic and Storm's life goals were to push for greater heights financially. Things were lovely and getting better by the day.

Strolling her way up to the room, she entered and quickly headed to the kitchen. Fixing her a glass of champagne, Storm took down the sweet Moet within a few sips.

"Dominic?" she called out. "I'm home, baby."

Walking through the large living area, she checked both rooms and didn't find her child or husband. Making her way down to the lobby, Storm walked outside and headed down to the boardwalk. The waves in the water drifted lightly on the shore as she made her way down to the sand.

Spotting Dominic standing with his feet in the water, Rain pranced around him with a bright beautiful smile that spelled baby fever. They looked like the best daddy and daughter to play on a Huggies commercial. Heading down by his side, she kissed his cheek and felt Rain grip ahold of her leg.

"How was your day?" Dominic asked, looking out at the water.

"It was great. The dealership is in full effect now and it's already off the ground. I think I'm going to like the business woman lifestyle. It makes me feel like a real boss." She smiled.

"Oh yeah? You're supposed to feel like a boss, because you are. Not to mention, look at who your husband is." He smirked before kissing her lips.

"Why are you teasing me?" she grinned, feeling her nookie tingle.

190

"I'm not. I've been waiting for you to get home. I think it's about time for my daily dosage."

"Mm-hmmmm. You sound very confident. How you know I ain't been waiting all day?"

"I'm quite sure you were. Before he could place another kiss on her lips, Storm pulled a white envelope from her back pocket. I have a surprise for you."

Looking at the envelope with a raised brow, Dominic smirked. "Is it tickets to the next Lakers game?" he cheesed.

"Open it and see."

Grabbing his surprise, Dominic quickly tore open the envelope and read the paper that rested inside. Watching his face change from a smile to a frown, he looked at Storm as if she was playing a trick on him.

"Is this real?" he questioned with a serious expression.

Smiling from ear to ear, Storm nodded her head. "That's correct. You're 99.99 percent Rain's father, according to your swab that I stole."

Dominic's eyes became watery, as he had a flashback of all the chaos his family was taken through. All of the blood that was spilled. It was all in vain. The life he chose to take care of was his biological seed the entire time and not once had it dawned on him to take a DNA test.

"I can't believe it," he mouthed before dropping to his knees in front of Rain. Wiping her father's tears, she pecked his lips and wrapped her tiny hands around his head.

Taking off her shoes, Storm wrapped them both in a hug and kissed Dominic's forehead. "So do you think you gave me everything I wanted?"

Looking up at her, he smiled. "Yes. I really do, baby and I thank you for showing me."

"It's my job," Storm replied before sitting with her family on the beach.

It was one thing she learned through her course. You can never stop what's meant to be, no matter how bad you try. The King family was on top and they still continued to grow happily ever after.

The End

Submission Guideline

Submit the first three chapters of your completed manuscript to <u>ldpsubmissions@gmail.com</u>, subject line: Your book's title. The manuscript must be in a .doc file and sent as an attachment. Document should be in Times New Roman, double spaced and in size 12 font. Also, provide your synopsis and full contact information. If sending multiple submissions, they must each be in a separate email.

Have a story but no way to send it electronically? You can still submit to LDP/Ca$h Presents. Send in the first three chapters, written or typed, of your completed manuscript to:

LDP: Submissions Dept
Po Box 870494
Mesquite, Tx 75187

DO NOT send original manuscript. Must be a duplicate.

Provide your synopsis and a cover letter containing your full contact information.

Thanks for considering LDP and Ca$h Presents.

Destiny Skai & Chris Green

Coming Soon from Lock Down Publications/Ca$h Presents

BOW DOWN TO MY GANGSTA
By **Ca$h**
TORN BETWEEN TWO
By **Coffee**
BLOOD STAINS OF A SHOTTA **III**
By **Jamaica**
STEADY MOBBIN **III**
By **Marcellus Allen**
RENEGADE BOYS IV
By Meesha
BLOOD OF A BOSS **VI**
SHADOWS OF THE GAME II
By **Askari**
LOYAL TO THE GAME **IV**
LIFE OF SIN **III**
By **T.J. & Jelissa**
A DOPEBOY'S PRAYER **II**
By **Eddie "Wolf" Lee**
IF LOVING YOU IS WRONG… **III**
By **Jelissa**
TRUE SAVAGE **VII**
By **Chris Green**
BLAST FOR ME **III**
DUFFLE BAG CARTEL **IV**
HEARTLESS GOON **II**

Married to a Boss… 3

By **Ghost**
A HUSTLER'S DECEIT III
KILL ZONE **II**
BAE BELONGS TO ME III
SOUL OF A MONSTER III
By **Aryanna**
THE COST OF LOYALTY **III**
By **Kweli**
A GANGSTER'S SYN III
By **J-Blunt**
KING OF NEW YORK V
RISE TO POWER III
COKE KINGS IV
BORN HEARTLESS II
By **T.J. Edwards**
GORILLAZ IN THE BAY IV
De'Kari
THE STREETS ARE CALLING II
Duquie Wilson
KINGPIN KILLAZ IV
STREET KINGS III
PAID IN BLOOD II
Hood Rich
SINS OF A HUSTLA II
ASAD
TRIGGADALE III
Elijah R. Freeman

195

Destiny Skai & Chris Green

KINGZ OF THE GAME IV

Playa Ray

SLAUGHTER GANG III

RUTHLESS HEART

By Willie Slaughter

THE HEART OF A SAVAGE II

By Jibril Williams

FUK SHYT II

By Blakk Diamond

THE DOPEMAN'S BODYGAURD II

By Tranay Adams

TRAP GOD

By Troublesome

YAYO II

By S. Allen

GHOST MOB

Stilloan Robinson

KINGPIN DREAMS

By Paper Boi Rari

CREAM

By Yolanda Moore

Available Now

RESTRAINING ORDER **I & II**

By **CA$H & Coffee**

LOVE KNOWS NO BOUNDARIES **I II & III**

By **Coffee**

RAISED AS A GOON I, II, III & IV

BRED BY THE SLUMS I, II, III

BLAST FOR ME I & II

ROTTEN TO THE CORE I II III

A BRONX TALE I, II, III

DUFFEL BAG CARTEL I II III

HEARTLESS GOON

A SAVAGE DOPEBOY

HEARTLESS GOON

By **Ghost**

LAY IT DOWN **I & II**

LAST OF A DYING BREED

BLOOD STAINS OF A SHOTTA I & II

By **Jamaica**

LOYAL TO THE GAME

LOYAL TO THE GAME II

LOYAL TO THE GAME III

LIFE OF SIN I, II

By **TJ & Jelissa**

BLOODY COMMAS I & II

SKI MASK CARTEL I II & III

KING OF NEW YORK I II,III IV

RISE TO POWER I II

COKE KINGS I II III

BORN HEARTLESS

By **T.J. Edwards**

Destiny Skai & Chris Green

IF LOVING HIM IS WRONG…I & II
LOVE ME EVEN WHEN IT HURTS I II III
By **Jelissa**
WHEN THE STREETS CLAP BACK I & II III
By **Jibril Williams**
A DISTINGUISHED THUG STOLE MY HEART I II & III
LOVE SHOULDN'T HURT I II III IV
RENEGADE BOYS I II III
By **Meesha**
A GANGSTER'S CODE I &, II III
A GANGSTER'S SYN II
By J-Blunt
PUSH IT TO THE LIMIT
By **Bre' Hayes**
BLOOD OF A BOSS **I, II, III, IV, V**
SHADOWS OF THE GAME
By **Askari**
THE STREETS BLEED MURDER **I, II & III**
THE HEART OF A GANGSTA I II& III
By **Jerry Jackson**
CUM FOR ME
CUM FOR ME 2
CUM FOR ME 3
CUM FOR ME 4
CUM FOR ME 5
An **LDP Erotica Collaboration**
BRIDE OF A HUSTLA **I II & II**

THE FETTI GIRLS **I, II& III**

CORRUPTED BY A GANGSTA I, II III, IV

BLINDED BY HIS LOVE

By **Destiny Skai**

WHEN A GOOD GIRL GOES BAD

By **Adrienne**

THE COST OF LOYALTY I II

By **Kweli**

A GANGSTER'S REVENGE **I II III & IV**

THE BOSS MAN'S DAUGHTERS

THE BOSS MAN'S DAUGHTERS II

THE BOSSMAN'S DAUGHTERS III

THE BOSSMAN'S DAUGHTERS IV

THE BOSS MAN'S DAUGHTERS **V**

A SAVAGE LOVE **I & II**

BAE BELONGS TO ME I II

A HUSTLER'S DECEIT I, II, III

WHAT BAD BITCHES DO I, II, III

SOUL OF A MONSTER I II

KILL ZONE

By **Aryanna**

A KINGPIN'S AMBITON

A KINGPIN'S AMBITION **II**

I MURDER FOR THE DOUGH

By **Ambitious**

TRUE SAVAGE

TRUE SAVAGE II

TRUE SAVAGE **III**

TRUE SAVAGE **IV**

TRUE SAVAGE **V**

TRUE SAVAGE **VI**

By **Chris Green**

A DOPEBOY'S PRAYER

By **Eddie "Wolf" Lee**

THE KING CARTEL **I, II & III**

By **Frank Gresham**

THESE NIGGAS AIN'T LOYAL **I, II & III**

By **Nikki Tee**

GANGSTA SHYT **I II &III**

By **CATO**

THE ULTIMATE BETRAYAL

By **Phoenix**

BOSS'N UP **I , II & III**

By **Royal Nicole**

I LOVE YOU TO DEATH

By Destiny J

I RIDE FOR MY HITTA

I STILL RIDE FOR MY HITTA

By **Misty Holt**

LOVE & CHASIN' PAPER

By **Qay Crockett**

TO DIE IN VAIN

SINS OF A HUSTLA

By **ASAD**

BROOKLYN HUSTLAZ

By **Boogsy Morina**

BROOKLYN ON LOCK I & II

By **Sonovia**

GANGSTA CITY

By **Teddy Duke**

A DRUG KING AND HIS DIAMOND I & II III

A DOPEMAN'S RICHES

HER MAN, MINE'S TOO I, II

CASH MONEY HO'S

By Nicole Goosby

TRAPHOUSE KING **I II & III**

KINGPIN KILLAZ I II III

STREET KINGS I II

PAID IN BLOOD

By **Hood Rich**

LIPSTICK KILLAH **I, II, III**

CRIME OF PASSION I & II

By **Mimi**

STEADY MOBBN' **I, II, III**

By **Marcellus Allen**

WHO SHOT YA **I, II, III**

Renta

GORILLAZ IN THE BAY **I II III**

DE'KARI

TRIGGADALE I II

Elijah R. Freeman

Destiny Skai & Chris Green

GOD BLESS THE TRAPPERS I, II, III
THESE SCANDALOUS STREETS I, II, III
FEAR MY GANGSTA I, II, III
THESE STREETS DON'T LOVE NOBODY I, II
BURY ME A G I, II, III, IV, V
A GANGSTA'S EMPIRE I, II, III, IV
THE DOPEMAN'S BODYGAURD
Tranay Adams
THE STREETS ARE CALLING
Duquie Wilson
MARRIED TO A BOSS… I II III
By Destiny Skai & Chris Green
KINGZ OF THE GAME I II III
Playa Ray
SLAUGHTER GANG I II
By Willie Slaughter
THE HEART OF A SAVAGE
By Jibril Williams
FUK SHYT
By Blakk Diamond
DON'T F#CK WITH MY HEART I II
By Linnea
ADDICTED TO THE DRAMA I II III
By Jamila
YAYO
By S. Allen

202

BOOKS BY LDP'S CEO, CA$H

TRUST IN NO MAN

TRUST IN NO MAN 2

TRUST IN NO MAN 3

BONDED BY BLOOD

SHORTY GOT A THUG

THUGS CRY

THUGS CRY 2

THUGS CRY 3

TRUST NO BITCH

TRUST NO BITCH 2

TRUST NO BITCH 3

TIL MY CASKET DROPS

RESTRAINING ORDER

RESTRAINING ORDER 2

IN LOVE WITH A CONVICT

Coming Soon

BONDED BY BLOOD 2

BOW DOWN TO MY GANGSTA